DOLPHIN JOURNEY

DOLPHIN JOURNEY

Erin Anne Pyne

iUniverse, Inc.
New York Lincoln Shanghai

Dolphin Journey

iUniverse, Inc.

For information address:
iUniverse, Inc.
2021 Pine Lake Road, Suite 100
Lincoln, NE 68512
www.iuniverse.com

ISBN: 0-595-31406-6

Printed in the United States of America

For my beloved husband, Greg—your love and devotion are my inspiration.

Special Thanks to the other founders of the PenDragons.

"*To the dolphin alone, beyond all other, nature has granted what the best philosophers seek: friendship for no advantage.*"

—Plutarch

Contents

❀

Epic Form

An explosion of water erupted from the surface of the Pacific Ocean as a bottlenose dolphin leapt into the air. Her eyes were forward, scanning the distance for signs of circling sea gulls. Serena seemed to remain suspended in air for a moment as she spotted low flying birds, the tell-tale sign of a large school of fish. She ducked her head slightly, re-entering the water with perfect grace. She whistled to the other dolphins that she had spotted the gulls.

"Flyers, straight ahead! Hurry up everyone!"

The rest of the group behind her had to see for themselves, and all nine dolphins jumped with both eyes focused on the mob of sea gulls spiraling through the air. Serena was excited. This was the best moment of every day, the thrill of the hunt, and the rush of knowing her importance in the success of the group. She leaped in the air and felt her heart trying to jump out of her skin as her excitement grew.

As the group of dolphins closed in, they swam under water, casting sound waves outward to get an idea of the exact size and shape of the school. Alatina, the Matriarch, clicked orders at the rest of the dolphins. The other dolphins knew not to ignore her.

"Ana. Radill. Go left, now! Anu. Ravis. Go right. Surround the fish. Don't let them escape! Aleta, follow me. We'll go beneath them."

The other dolphins immediately followed orders, moving into their positions. Serena waited for her instructions, although she already new what her job would be.

"Serena, go topside. Make some noise!"

Serena leapt into the air as she reached the clump of fish, and landed with a loud smash back into the water. The fish panicked at the thunderous crack and swam into a protective ball. As if with one mind the fish turned from side to side like liquid silver, looking for an escape. The four dolphins, circling on the left and the right, kept the fish from breaking into small groups. Several fish broke from the main group in an attempt to swim past the dolphins. Bubbles streamed from the dolphins' blowholes as they shouted at the fish, scaring them back into the circle.

"I don't think so!" Radill cried as she swiped her tail towards the fleeing fish.

"Good save, Radill!" Aleta called from beneath her.

Serena concentrated on her job and continued to breach and slap down on the water in a circular pattern, confusing the fish and preventing the school from splitting apart. The fish were driven to the surface by Alatina and Aleta below. Two younger dolphins, Seris and Tinen, stayed close to the adults, watching and learning. The fish soon became exhausted. The dolphins were now able to begin eating, one at a time, without danger of the ball of fish breaking up. The sea gulls who had helped the dolphins find their prey, were now getting their rewards. From above, the birds now dove down to catch the fish in their spear-like beaks.

Serena looked at the dolphins below her. Alatina gave orders of who was to eat first. Serena waited for her turn.

"Serena, dive in!" Hearing the whistles, Serena plunged head first into the fish with her mouth wide open. During the beginning of the hunt the dolphins had made a racket of sound when casting sound waves towards to fish, keeping them in line. Now they were almost silent as each dolphin ate her fill by taking turns until the last fish was devoured. Serena felt tired, full, and absolutely content. She gobbled up the last fish, swallowing it down whole.

Serena was lean and strong. She had grey skin along her face and back, but her belly was pearl white. Serena had three light grey stripes on her melon and her face was lightly sprinkled with freckles. She had large, dark grey eyes.

Serena loved to hunt. It had always been her favorite game. Sometimes she treated hunting like a mystery, looking for clues as to where a creature is hiding, and following the trail to the hiding victim. She liked to pretend that she was a shark, stalking her prey silently, and then pouncing on it without warning. Sand blasting was one of her favorite hunting games. By echolocating a sound beam into the sand, Serena found slippery fish, or scuttling crabs. They were very crunchy snacks.

The group leader, the matriarch, made Serena the scout because of her amazing ability to hunt and track. The dolphins celebrated the successful catch by commending Serena on her fine scouting and then lazily cruising around the shallow coasts.

"Serena!" Six alternating high and low pitched whistles met Serena's ears and she immediately recognized her own name. The matriarch was calling her.

"Coming, Alatina."

Alatina was an older female; she was a dark gray with old battle scars to prove she was the leader. Serena bolted towards her, and was met with a flurry of whistles and trills.

"Fly ahead, Serena. Report back the cause of that sound. Do you hear it?"

Serena turned her head in the direction Alatina was facing. Through her fatty lower jaw she perceived a very low rumble. She took off fast, and jumped low and long above the water, able to move more quickly in the air. The hunt had led the dolphins into more shallow waters, and Serena had a good idea what was making the noise. The sound became louder and her casting revealed an enormous skywhale.

She called the object a skywhale because it looked like the upside-down backbone of a whale, covered with hard skin that moved across the surface of the water. It was a large boat. This time her leap was for joy. Serena squeaked in her excitement, knowing she'd be getting a good ride. She turned back enough to let Alatina know of her find, and raced to catch the giant ship that pushed the waves. Serena knew some of the females would not be riding because of the calves, but she was ready for some fun.

Swimming up along side, she caught the slipstream of the ship and glided easily along. Pushing ahead, Serena jumped into the bow wave that pushed her forward with excellent force. She whistled and giggled, gleefully propelling through the water. She occasionally looked upward at the animals on the skywhale, the slowspeakers. They looked down at her pointing, and sometimes reaching down with their long spindly arms at her. The only other creatures she knew of with arms were types of sea bugs.

She had never heard them speak, but the older dolphins sang of the creatures that spoke, but with such slow sound frequencies, no one could possibly understand them. Dolphin language is fast, very fast. In a few short chirps they can communicate an entire sentence or idea. A human listening to a dolphin might only hear a whistle, but the dolphins would hear many sounds and pitches.

"Hey, Serena! Good find!" Aleta joined Serena and they jumped through the waves, giggling as young dolphins do. Anu joined them as well, and all three dolphins moved as one through the waves.

"Do you see the slowspeakers up there?" Serena glanced up at the people.

"Yeah," Aleta replied. "Strange creatures. But they seem intelligent enough, almost as smart as me."

Serena chuffed. Anu squeaked through the rushing water, "They seem harmless enough. As long as you watch the skywhale spinners."

Serena remembered her mother telling her about the dangerous part of a skywhale. The spinner, the propeller. Serena felt pain as she thought about her mother, but she couldn't stop herself from remembering a lesson about riding skywhales and watching out for the spinner by veering away from the skywhale before turning around.

'Very good, Serena. Having fun?'

'Yeah, Mom. I love riding the skywhales!'

'Alright, now the trick is being able to leave the bow wave safely. You must avoid the spinner at all costs. Skywhales are fun, but can be dangerous too. There are two sides to everything.'

'Yeah, Mom. I know. I'm ready.'

'All right, on the count of three swim off to the right and wait for the skywhale to pass before turning. One, two, three!'

Serena glanced around at her nursery mates. Aleta and Anu had been born during the same year as Serena, five cycles ago. They grew up together and had never been apart. Serena read their body language and the girls predicted each others' behaviors so well they didn't need to signal to jump together anymore. Anu, who was the oldest of the three, made a point to push Serena out of a good wave.

"What was that for?" challenged Serena, swerving back into the bow wave.

Anu ignored her, however, so Serena dropped it. The three dolphins sped together through the salty water in silence enjoying the sensations, but they knew they must not stay for long or they would be too far ahead of the others. After one more leap they veered off together and swam back to the group.

"Serena," greeted Alatina. "Which direction was the skywhale headed?"

"Towards the shallows, into shore."

Alatina surfaced and took a deep breath before she spoke again. "All the skywhales have been heading that way today. No skywhales have been going out. That is unusual."

Alatina swam away. Serena did not question Alatina. She often swam alone to think. Thinking and planning ahead was part of being a matriarch. Taking care of the nursery was her job.

Serena had lived with this group of dolphins her entire life, five cycles. The beginning of another cycle approached as the females prepared to give birth. Serena looked toward her friend, Ravis, who had lived seven cycles, and used echolocation toward her large belly. Serena created a rapid train of clicks by contracting muscles just below her blowhole. The clicks concentrated into a beam of sound through her melon, and Serena aimed the beam of sound, casting Ravis's belly. As the sound wave bounced back from Ravis, Serena caught it through her lower jaw. From this sound wave Serena saw a picture in her mind of the baby Ravis was carrying inside her.

"Your calf will be healthy, playful, and wise." Serena squeaked to Ravis.

"You say that to every mother about her calf, Serena."

"That is because it is true, every calf is healthy, playful, and wise; or it is not long in the world."

"I hope I have a girl," Ravis squeaked swimming in circles around Serena. "If I do I'll name it after you, Serena."

Serena blew out a stream of bubbles form her blowhole. "No! You mustn't! You must name her after Radill, your mother. Name her Radisa."

"What would you name your calf, Serena?"

"My calf! I'm only five. I won't have my first calf for at least two cycles or longer."

The dolphins swam together to the surface taking a breath at the same time. "Well, that gives you plenty of time to think of a name."

Serena's home range was the southern half of the Gulf of California, also called the Sea of Cortez. The gulf was located between the Baja Peninsula of California and Mexico. The dolphins called it BrightWater. Many species of cetaceans called BrightWater home, such as common and bottlenose dolphins. Bryde's whales, humpback, gray, short-finned pilot, and killer whales all took advantage of these food rich waters. Even the largest animal on Earth visited this paradise, as blue whale mother and calf pairs often swam here, with dolphins riding their wake. Manta rays fed here on the plentiful plankton, and fish were colorful and numerous. Large coral reefs created a playground for the dolphins. Serena had always lived in BrightWater. She had never been anywhere else. She felt safe here and she never grew tired of the beauty that surrounded her.

Darkness was falling upon the ocean and everyone needed to be together during the Black. Dolphins call night time the Black because that is what it is, pitch-blackness. The only light came from the moon, and a few feet below the surface that light was completely blocked out. It was almost like going completely blind for ten hours. During the Black dolphins only had one way to see the ocean around them, their echolocation. Throughout the night the dolphins would be casting their sound waves to look for sharks.

"Gather around, everyone," trilled Alatina. Alatina was singing a song as Serena, Anu, and Aleta stopped their game of flip the sea star. The song was part of the Epic. Tinen, Alatina's one year calf, was bugging Serena with questions about the skywhale.

"Was it fun, how did it feel? I've only ridden the little skywhales. I can't wait to ride the big ones!"

"Hush, Tinen. Alatina is about to sing an Epic."

"Epic? What's an Epic?"

"Tinen! You know what Epic's are. The Epic is the song of life. It is the song of nature."

"Is Mom's Epic the only one?"

"Of course not. There are many Epics. Some Epics are known by all dolphins throughout the seas. Some are known only to dolphins in a specific home range. Some Epics are only known to small groups, like our nursery. Some are only shared from mother to calf. You will know Epic's from Alatina that no one else knows, Tinen."

"Wow!" Tinen trilled.

"Now hush up and listen." Serena turned her attention to Alatina, who had already begun to sing. Alatina's Epic explained that the world supported different creatures, and each life supported another. The Epic contained many high and low squeaks, long whistles, and short trills. The other dolphins responded to favorite passages by leaping or whistling their names.

Alatina sang,

> Our friendship is an energy that flows through each of us. Energy can never be destroyed. It can only change forms. The energy of your life will be strong forever in your bonds with each other. You and the water are one with each other; your beauty is the same beauty of the entire natural world. All are one. Our energy will pass through all that lives in the Oceans.

The nine dolphins were silent a moment, than clicked and whistled at these words while rubbing Alatina on her back and flippers in admiration of her wisdom.

Ravis and Serena rubbed flippers and Serena buzzed Ravis with a sound casting as if to say goodnight to the calf. They paired up for the Black tonight and Serena shut one of her eyes to rest. She came up to the surface to breathe every once in a while. Serena looked with one eye up into the night sky and gazed at the stars.

She did not wonder about them, she only accepted that they were there. Serena's curiosity did not surpass the here and now. She was curious, but did not question the origins of things. She did not wonder what stars were made from, or ask where they came from. Dolphins may have a soul, but they would never think of it.

Serena ducked down below the surface and echolocated into the dark water. She noticed Tinen swimming too far from Alatina. She focused her echolocation in his direction, and as the echo came back to Serena she got a picture in her mind. Tinen's small body was motionless. He had frozen and had his tail to Serena.

"Tinen?" Serena chirped. He did not respond.

She broadened her echo cast into the darkness and saw that directly in front of Tinen was a large shark! Serena gave out a shrill cry and all the dolphins became aware of what was going on.

"Shark! Shark!"

"Tinen, Seris, come by me!" Alatina whistled sharply.

Tinen, who had frozen when he saw the shark, raced under his mother who was ready to protect him with her life. Seris swam under Alatina too. Radill, Ana, Anu, Aleta, and Serena formed a line between the shark and the other dolphins. Serena clapped her jaws together making a loud popping sound towards the shark. The other dolphins postured aggressively towards it.

Serena barked at the intruder, "Get out of here or we're going to tear you apart!" All the dolphins jaw popped, sending ear piercing bangs through the water. The shark must have realized his attempt at stealth had been detected because he turned tail and fled. Serena and Aleta chased him to make sure he got the point.

"He was no match for us." Serena bubbled. "He won't be coming back."

"I'm glad you were paying attention, Serena." Aleta whistled. "Tinen must have been too scared to call out."

Serena rubbed flippers with Aleta for a job well done. Serena felt satisfied with herself after standing up to such a dangerous predator. She thought that sharks were pretty cowardly once they were confronted. No shark would dare try to fight five healthy dolphins. Serena felt safe in her nursery. She knew others would fight for her, as she would fight for them.

The next morning, Serena began scouting the area. There was nothing of any significance to be reported, except that she felt a slight change in the tidal currents. Alatina felt it too. She took the change as a serious warning.

"Come everyone, we will need to make a great travel today. The water is in the beginnings of a great turmoil. In several Blacks the water will surge. All the signs are showing it. The current has changed; the skywhales are leaving the water. We need to leave."

The dolphins squeaked in opposition. Serena couldn't believe what she was hearing. Leave the nursery waters? Leave BrightWater? Where will they go? Serena swam over to Ravis who seemed worried at the news.

"Ravis, Ravis." Serena called.

She whistled back. "This is my first calf, Serena. You know many first mothers do not have good calves. How will mine do if I am too stressed? Traveling now? Where will we go?"

"Hush, now, Ravis. Alatina knows where we'll go. She knows that you will not be safe here if the waters move too forcefully. We'll go to a new nursery point. Oh, Alatina is calling me."

Serena left her friend and joined Alatina who had already begun swimming south. She moved into formation alongside Alatina with her oldest daughter, Aleta, just behind them.

"Serena, swim ahead and cast for other dolphins. Others will know about the storm and we'll be better off traveling with them."

"Yes, Alatina. May Aleta scout with me?"

Alatina thought a moment and decided it would not hurt the group. Two scouts might even help with relations in joining the larger companies.

"Alright, be back before the sun is directly overhead. If you encounter any trouble, you come right back."

Aleta and Serena squeaked an agreement. Anu swam over having heard the conversation.

"I should go too, after all, I am the best swimmer, and I've had experience with our group contacts."

"Only because she got lost when she was three and followed the wrong dolphin school for two hours," Aleta silently buzzed to Serena.

Alatina wasn't paying attention to Aleta, however, and allowed Anu to go. Together the three of them swam off ahead of the group. Serena leaped out of the water and dove perfectly back down barely creating a splash.

"See anything?" bubbled Anu.

"Nothing ahead but clear blue."

Serena's echolocation casting showed her nothing more than the depth of the ocean and the shape of the coral and the movement of the fish in front of her.

Aleta chirped, "The fish know something's up. They're moving funny, all jerky and afraid."

Anu chuffed, "Fish are afraid of everything; they are the jumpiest creatures alive. You just look at them and they freak out."

"Hey, check this out," Serena cried, "A ray!"

A brown stingray glided across the sandy floor minding its own business when the three playful dolphins started harassing it.

"Watch its stinger, Aleta." Serena warned.

Aleta was careful and grabbed the ray by the tip of its tail so that the stinger, located at the base of the tail near the body, couldn't reach her. Aleta dragged the poor stingray to the surface and tossed it into the air like a stingray frisbee. The ray hit the water and was stunned. Anu snagged it and with a flick of her head she tossed it even further. Aleta chased Anu, who held the ray in her mouth.

The game lasted a few more minutes and then Serena gave a sharp loud whistle. "Come here, girls. What is that?"

Aleta, who had managed to steal the ray back, dropped the harassed ray who instantly swam to the ocean bottom and buried itself. The three girls looked like bobbing corks as they kept their heads above the water looking at the giant, loud object above them. A helicopter flew overhead in the direction the three dolphins had been headed.

"The slowspeakers travel in those. I've seen them inside." Serena said.

"The currents are getting stronger. I think we should go back to the school." Anu declared. "We haven't found any other dolphins yet," squeaked Serena. "We can't go back without news. Let's swim as far as we can before mid-light. I'll try calling other dolphin herds. Then we'll go back."

Aleta and Anu agreed and swam through the blue following Serena. Serena sent out long, low calls that would travel some distance, hopefully to be heard by others.

The morning was passing quickly and there were no signs of other dolphins nearby. Serena and the other two dolphins decided to head back to their own nursery. The sun was directly overhead when the dolphins reunited, and although Serena had little to report, Alatina had news.

"I contacted another group. They were heading north. They were going to try to outrun the storm instead of heading away from its path. We will travel south together. I don't want to split up anymore."

Alatina swam in the lead. Some of the older dolphins, Radill and Ana, were beside her. Ravis, Aleta, and Anu swam behind them. Serena swam with the two younger dolphins. Seris, from the same mother as Serena, was a three year old male. Tinen was Alatina's male calf from last year. Serena never knew who her father was and didn't know who Seris's father was. But they shared the same mother. Only females raise dolphin calves. The males are usually kept away from the young for safety. Male dolphins can be very violent in play and dominance displays. Serena took over caring for Seris two years ago when their mother died.

Serena did not know why her mother, Siren, had died. She had been growing weaker and weaker, stopped eating, and finally left the nursery forever. Alatina had gone with her to the shallows, and Siren went onto the beach to die peacefully. The only reason Seris had survived was because Serena cared for him so well. She had been very attentive and made sure he learned to eat fish quickly. He had nursed for almost a year before his mother had died, but normally he might have continued nursing for another year. All the females in the school helped raise Seris, but it was Serena who built the strongest bond.

"Serena! What's going on? Come on tell me! Are we moving a long distance? We haven't eaten yet today, and I'm hungry."

"I'm hungry too," squeaked Tinen.

"Tinen, if you're hungry go to Alatina and nurse," said Serena.

Tinen zipped up to his mother, prodding the mammary slits under her belly, hoping to get milk. Alatina, not wanting to be bothered at that moment, snapped at him, sending Tinen back to Serena who calmly chirped, "Well, maybe later, Tinen. She has a lot of planning to do."

Seris dove down and jaw popped at some fish who easily escaped capture.

"Seris, just wait. Alatina will tell us when and where to hunt. We'll get our fill. But we must get out of the way of the storm."

Nevertheless, Serena cast sound waves to the sand below, looking for an easy target.

The dolphins traveled in silence for a while. Serena trusted Alatina completely. She was sure that Alatina had traveled this way before and that her memory of the path was clear. Serena, Aleta, and Anu swam along side of her listening to one of her lessons.

"When storms begin to brew, the winds blow, and the blowing winds cause water movement. The movements of the waters tell us where the storm is coming from and where it is going. Feel the movement. Concentrate on direction, and you will be able to find your way." Serena tried to concentrate and feel the direction of storm. She still didn't understand how Alatina knew where to go, even if she knew where the storm was going. And figuring out how fast the storm was coming was still a mystery to Serena. But Alatina seemed to know that time was short. The dolphins continued swimming without stopping for hours.

Finally, Alatina stopped in clear, shallow waters. "We'll hunt here."

After a few seconds of casting Serena knew why. The sand was teeming with hiding fish. It was the perfect place for sand blasting. Ana was the first to begin serious hunting. She assumed a vertical position with her tail pointed up to the surface. The older female cast into the sand sending down powerful sound waves that would not only tell her where the fish were, but stun them just enough for her to dig down in the sand with her jaws and snatch up the fish. The other dolphins, having learned this behavior long ago, also directed their heads down towards the ocean floor in an upside down posture. They echolocated the fish and scooped them up with their jaws, crushing them and then swallowing them down whole.

Serena had eaten almost fifteen fish when she looked up and noticed that Seris was no longer next to her. She swam up to the surface and looked below her. She saw no sign of him. She quickly sent out a call. The other dolphins looked up and realized that Seris was gone. They echolocated the waters. Serena cast sound waves in a long range search pattern. Nothing, he was nowhere. It was as if he'd just disappeared.

Aleta must have been thinking the same thing. "This is impossible!" cried Aleta. "How did he just disappear?"

"Dolphins do not disappear," Alatina calmly said to her daughter. "He is not far. We will find him. Everyone, use your senses and Seris will be found."

Serena cast around her. She couldn't see him anywhere. There was nothing around besides a sandy bottom and piles of rocks. The other adults had already begun looking for him.

"Anu," Alatina commanded, "Take Tinen and go to the surface. Wait for Seris to come for a breath. You three follow me," addressing Serena, Aleta, and Ravis. "We don't have much time."

The four dolphins sped along the sandy ocean floor reaching a dip in the plain. This was a rocky region, with fish darting in and out of the crevices. Serena closed her eyes and listened.

She was surrounded with sound. Noise filled the ocean, from the songs and noises of other dolphins and whales, the wash of the waves, the moving undersea currents, the chatter of fish mouthing the rocks and coral, the crackle of shrimp, and sliding of sand. Serena blocked out the sounds of the sea and listened only for familiar sounds of Seris.

Suddenly she heard him. Seris was somewhere close, and he was screaming. His distress call filled the waters; three high pitched whistles that swooped up in pitch.

"Save, save, save!"

Serena called out his name and frantically echolocated around her. What if a shark had got him and was carrying him away! Then she realized that he was below her somehow. The others were searching all around the water, but Serena looked down to the rocks. She was getting desperate. Seris needed air now. His screams were filling the water around her and she couldn't tell where they were coming from until she saw the large boulder in front of her. She zipped around to the other side and saw a large opening. She echolocated inside the cave and saw her brother! He was a few feet in and he was stuck! Seris was in an awkward position. His tail was bent up against the rocks and his body was folded. It looked as if he went in the cave and tried to turn around but didn't make it. Serena clicked at him and he desperately clicked back. Serena didn't know what to do. She needed a way to pull him out. She looked down and found a long old piece of coral. She picked it up with her mouth, and without a thought for her own safety she swam head first into the hole. She was almost nose to nose with Seris.

"Grab this thing, and I'll pull you out."

Seris opened his mouth and clamped on to the coral end. Serena squiggled around to get out backward. Swimming backward is very difficult. Serena thrashed violently pushing backwards with her pectoral flippers, and Seris finally moved a few inches forward. He was nearly free and beat his tail hard against the rocks.

Finally, Seris was freed. He pushed Serena the rest of the way out of the cave, and the two of them raced to the surface to breathe.

"Where did you find him?" whistled Alatina.

Serena told the story and then Seris explained how he got trapped in the first place.

"Well, I was hunting with the rest of you when I saw a crab, so I started to follow it and…" the girls were clicking disapprovingly.

"Well I followed it into the cave over there, but I went too far in, so I tried to turn around but it wasn't big enough for me."

Seris's tail had bright red cuts where the rocks had scraped him. Anu swam over.

"You little runt, that sure was stupid swimming into a cave. But then I would expect it, stupidity runs in families."

Ana, Anu's mother, grunted. Serena spun toward Anu as Alatina jaw popped at Ana.

"What do you mean by that, Anu?"

Serena flexed her tail muscles to show Anu her power. Anu backed down from the challenge and swam behind her mother, Ana.

"Alright," said Alatina, "We don't have time for this, we've lost enough time already. We've got to hurry now the storm is nearly upon us."

The dolphins agreed and started swimming in silence as fast as they could toward the south. Seris gave Serena a fin rub as a thank you.

The storm was beginning to pick up. The flyers had all left the skies. The fish were hiding in their tiny shelters. Serena had not seen a skywhale throughout the entire day of traveling. Alatina was whistling for them to speed up. Serena was becoming tired from swimming fast for so long.

"What's the matter, Serena, too weak to make it?" Anu gave a long raspberry.

"Go beach yourself, Anu." Serena calmly replied, speeding up.

"Oh, like your mom did? No thanks, I don't want to be hunted and eaten." Anu had a nasty glint in her eye.

"What is that supposed to mean? And don't EVER talk about my mother!"

Serena turned sharply, stopping dead still in front of Anu her jaws open menacingly.

"Hey, don't be angry at me, it's the slowspeakers you should be upset with."

"Anu!" It was Alatina. "Go to the head of the group, now!"

Anu swam off towards the front to her mother. Serena was fuming. She couldn't believe Alatina was allowing her to get away with this! Siren and Alatina had been close friends. Why would Alatina allow Anu to make up wild stories? The currents suddenly whipped up with strength. Serena continued swimming alongside Alatina who was silent. It wasn't a normal silence. Serena knew Alatina was thinking about what Anu had said. Serena hoped Alatina would tell her what Anu was talking about. She didn't have time just now, however. Black was coming. Serena paired up with the still shaken Seris for the night.

CHAPTER 2

Water Wind

The dolphins raced through the heavy currents to escape the underwater storm. As Serena surfaced to take a breath she felt the tumultuous wind whipping through the sky. The ocean surface was a deadly combination of crashing waves and surges of water that the dolphins had difficulty swimming through. After another breath Serena dove down with the others trying to stay below the surface chaos. Seris stayed close to Serena. He was a strong swimmer for his size, but Serena was worried about him.

"Stay near me, Seris," Serena said with a chirp.

"I'm fine, we've been diving in storms before," Seris proclaimed confidently.

"I know," Serena clicked, "But this storm feels different to me. I don't recognize these current patterns."

Alatina and Tinen headed for the surface together for a breath and Seris followed them. Alatina actually seemed nervous, which made everyone nervous.

"Alatina, do you want me to scout ahead? I could hopefully find…"

"No, we must not split up. This storm has come faster than I thought it would. The currents are stronger than I had thought too."

Serena looked up as she took a breath. The sky was dark and gray. The ocean floor was being kicked around so much that visibility was only a couple feet. Serena was constantly casting to be able to follow the others. The sound echoes showed her that Alatina was leading with Tinen at her side. Behind her were the older females, Radill and Ana, with Ravis, Aleta, and Anu close behind. Seris was just behind Serena and she snapped at him to speed up. She quickly moved behind him and pushed him forward with a powerful nudge from her beak.

"Alright, I'm going!" squeaked Seris.

He zipped ahead to join the adults and stayed in the middle of the group. The entire school rose up together to breath. At the surface the storm was intensifying.

Whistling sharply, Alatina cried, "Change direction, head away from the shore, we don't want to get beached!"

Serena briefly imagined the horror of being stranded on land and fear propelled her and the rest of the nursery group onward through the raging waters. They had been swimming for what seemed like a midlight. Serena and the rest of the dolphins were becoming worn out.

"How much farther until we are out of this?" cried Ravis. "I'm worried the stress could injure my calf."

Alatina was wise and had experienced these circle storms before. "We are almost out, but the worst is at the edges of the storm, so everyone be careful."

Serena swam behind Seris not letting him slow down.

"Serena."

She knew it was Anu beside her.

"Serena, don't be afraid."

"I'm not afraid!" Serena whistled with a high pitch.

"Your mother was afraid when they took her away."

"Shut up, Anu, you're lying!"

Serena knew Anu wasn't as strong as her, the only way she could express her dominance was to upset her by lying. She tried to hold back her fury, but Anu kept pushing.

"The slowspeakers picked her up off the beach and carried her off."

"Anu, I'm going to give you a blast if you don't shut your hole! You didn't see her!"

"Oh, but I did see. Two years ago. Alatina saw it too. They took her, and they killed her."

"NO!"

Serena was in a rage. She turned, but Anu had already sped away towards her mother. Serena's mind was racing with images and stories she'd heard from other dolphins about humans taking dolphins from the beach. Why hadn't Alatina come to stop the fight? Why wasn't she saying that Anu was lying? Her heart was pounding and she raced forward to catch up with Alatina. She had to know if Anu was telling the truth. She was so distracted by her storm of emotions she was not aware the edge of the hurricane had stirred up the water causing vast swells.

Serena surfaced for a quick breath and a huge surge caught her and pushed her backwards almost head over tail. She tumbled through the water feeling the waves crashing into her body. Opening her eyes, Serena fought to regain control. She powered her way forward but realized the surface was rising farther and farther away. Serena was caught in a whirlpool of water that was pulling her down, down, where everything was black. The water was thick with debris and Serena closed her eyes, trying to concentrate. She echolocated around her but nothing comforting reached her. She only heard Alatina whistling sharply in the distance. Dark and disorienting, the ocean pulled down on Serena as she powered upward. In her panic she thought only of the surface, air, breathing. It seemed the harder she pushed, the farther down she fell. She continued trying to swim up to the surface for a long time. She was becoming exhausted. Serena had been underwater far too long as the mad water spun her in all directions. She was desperate for a breath. Serena changed directions, going against her instincts, and decided to swim downward with the water flow.

Serena regained control and swam out of the whirling current to the side. She swam like a bullet to the surface. Serena blasted out of the water and breathed a sweet relieving breath. She crashed down, but immediately popped her head above the surface. The hard rain and wind made seeing and hearing anything impossible. The waves caused by the intense wind were enormous swells, blocking her vision. She dipped down underwater and echolocated in all directions. Nothing. No sign of her nursery anywhere. She wondered how far the currents had taken her. Serena thought a moment about which direction she should go, and determined to swim diagonally through the oncoming currents. She hoped that was where her nursery family was headed.

After a while the water calmed and Serena once again spy hopped to survey her location. As the group scout she was well practiced in being on her own, surveying, and reporting back to the group. She looked around above water and could not see land or any flyers. The rain was now a light sprinkle but she saw more dark clouds ahead. Serena cast all around her. The water, normally green and clear, was stirred up with dirt and plants making searching with sight useless. Serena clicked and whistled hoping her nursery was not far. The sun had moved completely across the sky and still she had contacted no one.

"Where is everyone?"

She wandered in the eerie emptiness of the sea. It seemed all the animals had left BrightWater. The remaining fish were hiding in their holes or under the sand. Serena hoped her nursery was alright. Serena suddenly feared that they may have been hurt in the storm.

"Alatina!" Serena called. "Alatina! I'm here!"

Serena felt very nervous. How far away could they be? Finally, she heard distant clicks and buzzes. She swam in that direction and cast other dolphins not too far away. Serena jumped out of the water landed with a great smack. That would let them know where she was, and that she was all right.

She sped toward the group and realized only as she approached that this was not her nursery family. This was a huge super herd of dolphins traveling together. There were over fifty dolphins swimming in the company. Males, females, and calves, the old and the young, were traveling together to escape the storm. Serena called out her name, but no one answered. She echolocated hoping to catch a glimpse of a familiar dolphin. Serena could easily recognize any of her nursery dolphins at a glance. Her school was not among this group. She entered the massive company of dolphins near the front introducing herself with her signature whistle, six alternating high and low pitched chirps.

A young male approached her and greeted her with a buzz to show friendship. Serena excitedly responded to his acceptance with a side rub.

"I'm Neo," he said with four high chirps. "Is your school lost?"

"What?" Serena cocked her head to the side, confused.

"Well, you're here with us, so we know where *you* are. If your school isn't with you, they must be lost."

Serena chuffed, "As if Alatina could get lost."

"Your mother?"

"My matriarch!" Serena barked back at him.

"Alright, sorry. Don't get upset." Serena was irritated but she swam alongside Neo anyway.

"Where is your school?" Serena chirped. Serena wasn't sure if Neo had already left his nursery family to join groups of males in alliances.

"I...I don't have an alliance yet," Neo quietly whistled. He swam silently beside Serena for a while.

"I'm five, I am the scout for my nursery," Serena tried to start a conversation.

"I'm six." Neo responded excitedly.

Serena looked at him out of the corner of her eye. He had grey freckles on his white belly and on his chin. His melon had two light grey lines and one dark line running down the middle. His dorsal fin was a nice curve along the front, but the back edge had three small notches. He also had three small notches on his right fluke.

He liked to chirp so Serena was silent as he explained the situation.

"The storm was huge. The air moved in a great circle, the currents were very strong. We all joined up to escape. Other groups joined us as we headed south. We're all going down to the warmer waters until the storm is completely gone."

Other dolphins swam about Serena to inspect the newcomer. They stayed shallow for easy access to the air with such large numbers of dolphins around them. The sky opened and poured water down onto the sea creating a thunderous hammer under water.

Serena continued calling for the other members of her school but no one answered. She was becoming tired and knew she would need to rest soon. Serena did not go fully unconscious when she slept. Only half her brain sleeps, the other half stays awake. Serena closed one eye but continued to be aware of the dolphins around her. For a moment Serena put aside her fears for her friends and family to rest her mind. She absently thought about where the school was headed and how many Blacks would pass before she could return home.

Serena was brought back to full consciousness by a jab in her side. She barked at the perpetrator who turned out to be Neo.

He circled her squeaking, "Get up! Get up!"

"Hey! What are you doing?!" chirped Serena.

"You better swim, Serena, because we're all coming to get you."

Serena looked behind her with her left eye and saw four other juvenile dolphins swimming straight for her, buzzing like mad. Serena's eyes grew wide as she realized a game of chase was about to begin and she was the first target!

"Go, go, go!" Neo barked, and Serena took off like a flash through the water.

Neo and the others immediately increased their speed with the escape attempt and the game was on. Serena sped through the murky sea, her echolocation buzzing ahead of her. She turned an eye back to see the others right on her tail. She leaped into the cold rain followed by the others who leaped with her. She re-entered the water at a sharp angle, dove down, and changed direction. Serena, like other dolphins, was an accomplished swimmer. She could turn in an instant at sharp angles allowing her to turn around head to tail in a fraction of a second. She could stop instantly, even at top speeds. The others were diving after her, so Serena turned around to face straight up in a surprise move. Some dolphins continued to speed right past her while others stopped cold. She quickly gained momentum and shot forward through the group who whistled and mouthed at her. Neo was the first to catch up with her on the way to the surface.

"I'm gonna catch you! Let's see how well you fly!" he shrilly cried.

Serena chuffed at him playfully and darted out of the water. Neo flew up into the air and flipped his tail toward Serena as she spun in a full 360° spin. Both crashed down ungracefully into the water and the game was suddenly over. The other young dolphins joined the main company and Serena joined them. A couple young girls approached whistling their names. Two long whistles for Ridge, and three short trills for Relm. Serena whistled her name with six alternating high and low whistles.

"I'm Serena. Are you all of one nursery?"

"Yes," replied the one who called herself Ridge.

Ridge had dark grey skin with three dark lines running down her melon. Her dorsal fin looked wavy along the back edge, and her tail flukes had a notch, probably from getting bit by another dolphin.

The young female who whistled her name as Relm clicked, "We are from the same nursery group. Our mothers are just behind us. Where is your nursery?"

"I'm not sure. We were separated in the storm."

"Oh no!" squeaked a young calf.

"I'm sure I'll find them. Alatina will easily locate and join the migration. So, find anything good to eat?"

The girls agreed that food was what they should be talking about, so the calf went to nurse from its mother while Serena, Neo, Ridge, and Relm scanned the water and floor for snacks.

CHAPTER 3

Invisible Walls

As Black came Serena paired with the girls. The large herd of dolphins continued to travel all night long and all day the next day. Many of the dolphins had eaten only bits that they had come across. The large school needed to hunt. The next morning Serena watched curiously as a group of older females swam together at the front of the group. It was some of the matriarchs. She swam up close enough to overhear their conversation.

"We need to find a large fish school soon. We've been picking on sea cucumbers and crabs the last few days and its time to eat fish."

"Tonina, we cannot split the company to search for fish. We will continue on the main path and eat what is available."

"The company cannot go on without a good meal!"

"Do you want the storm to catch us again?!"

"LADIES!"

The largest of the females barked at the others and popped her jaw making a cracking sound. Serena jerked in surprise.

"Listen to me, all of you! This school will not break up. We will send scouts to forage ahead. Only when they find food will we deviate from our course."

"I do not agree, Pryor!" the matriarch Tonina challenged. "We will search this area for food now!"

The matriarch Pryor flipped her tail up Tonina. She responded by jawing and lowering her front flippers. The other dolphins in the area crowded around to watch the fight. Pryor raked her sharp teeth across Tonina's back leaving four marks behind. Serena winced knowing how rakes felt as she'd gotten plenty from her disciplining mother. Pryor roughly shoved her hard beak into the soft side of the other matriarch. A short chase ensued but the Pryor was the more dominant in the end. She called her school to her and sent two scouts for food. Serena wanted to go with them but did not dare challenge the new matriarch of the company.

The sun was nearing halfway overhead when the scouts returned and the herd raced in the direction of apparently a large school of fish. Serena was ready for the hunt. Her blood pumped in her excitement and she had to swim at the surface allowing excess heat to escape off her dorsal fin. She was excited about being a part of such a large hunting group. Nothing would escape from them.

"Neo, you ready for the hunt?"

"Yeah, Serena. I'm so hungry, I'll eat an entire school by myself."

"Hey, save some for me!" Ridge chirped as she joined up with Neo and Serena.

"Where is Relm?" Serena trilled.

"She's swimming with her mother." Serena looked sideways over at Ridge. "I know she's a bit old, but they still have a close bond."

Serena looked away. She had been close to her mother. They had been great friends. Serena was prevented from thinking about her mother as the company neared the hunt.

"That's strange," Ridge cocked her head to the side as she cast sound waves ahead. "There is no fish school ahead."

"What is it?" Neo questioned.

"Listen," Serena chuffed. "The rumbling."

They were headed for a skywhale! A loud one. Serena was confused as to why the matriarch had them attacking a skywhale. She popped up to see slow-speakers looking over the side of the skywhale, waving their long arms and making muffled sounds. The fifty dolphins followed the back of the big sky-whale as it rumbled louder, and sped up away from them across the choppy waters. Only then did Serena realize the reason the scouts had brought every-one here.

Piles of shrimp flowed into the water from the back of the skywhale. Serena, Neo, and Ridge eagerly snapped at them, gulping down the shrimp. The other dolphins were taking advantage of this easy meal as well. Serena cast forward to find out the source of the bounty. The shrimp were being dragged behind the skywhale in a big circle, like a web of sea grasses. Each strand was very small and difficult to pick up through echolocation. She swam closer to get a better look. The skywhale was moving very fast now but with the flush of water keeping up was easy. Serena pushed her way forward chomping down shrimp as she went and saw that there was a big hole in the web-like strands, through which the shrimp were pouring out. The dolphins happily chirped and clicked as they fed upon the spilling shrimp. Suddenly the skywhale stopped and several dolphins attacked the net, tearing with their teeth to get at the shrimp.

The Mexican fisherman realized they were losing their shrimp catch and rushed to the side of the boat. Serena watched as the slowspeakers looked over the edge of the skywhale. They were making noise and waving their spindly arms around again. They reached down and started pulling the shrimp net out of the water. The dolphins continued to munch on as much shrimp as possible.

Suddenly a loud, piercing bang shot through the water. The sound was so loud it hurt Serena's jaw.

"Flee!" Pryor called. "A blaster!"

Serena immediately retreated from the boat with the other scattering dolphins. She corked up out of the water and saw a slowspeaker holding a black object in the air. Serena wondered if that small object made that loud of a noise. She could not have known the shrimp fisherman had used a gun to shoot a bullet into the water to scare off the dolphins. The slowspeakers pulled all the shrimp out of the water and then rumbled away. Serena had the feeling that they had been stealing the slowspeakers' kill. But she didn't really care. Stealing food is part of hunting. And she had eaten a very good meal. The dolphins celebrated the meal with leaps, dances, and rubs. The scouts were commended and the migration continued south toward warmer waters, away from the circle storm.

Serena caught up with Neo. "What was it that made the sound, Neo?"

"I don't know. Pryor called it a blaster."

"Well, that fits," Serena chirped. "That vibration was so loud, my melon shook."

Ridge swam up behind, hearing the conversation. "I think Pryor has hunted this way before. After all, she knew what a blaster was. My matriarch Tonina says she doesn't agree with skywhale scavenging."

Relm swam up to them. "Hey, that was great meal, wasn't it. Mother wasn't too happy though. She said it was too dangerous."

"Well," Serena turned to face the others. "Pryor is our company leader, so until something changes we'll have to follow her."

It wasn't long before everyone was hungry again. Hunting takes up most of a dolphin's life since the fish don't swim willing into the dolphins' mouths. Serena herself needed to eat at least twenty pounds of food every single day. She foraged the ocean bottom as the herd moved. She cast through the sand and under rocks to find the occasional fish or crab. Serena successfully snagged a fish that was hiding under the sand. She grabbed the fish in her teeth, and shook her head tearing the fish to kill it. She flipped the fish into her mouth, and as she swallowed, Serena pushed the salt water from her mouth with her tongue. She swallowed the fish whole and head first. All this took less than a second.

The next few days were uneventful, aside from the games of stingray frisbee and seaweed tag. Neo and Ridge had a fight over an octopus, but it squirted them both right it their faces and it escaped.

Relm was about Serena's age. She was the lightest in color of all of them, except that she had dark, smoky circles around her eyes, making her eyes look larger than they were. Relm and Serena became close over the next several days as they played together.

"Come on Relm, let's go swim to the front of the company. We can pretend we're matriarchs leading the group."

Relm hesitated. She loved to play, but she normally didn't stray far from her mother's watchful eyes.

"I don't know, Serena. I should probably stay close."

"Oh, come on. Tonina and your mother can cast you even if we're at the front."

Relm reluctantly agreed, but when she was at the front of the group, nothing in front of her but blue ocean, Relm forgot all about her fears.

"Matriarch Relm, which way will we be headed today?" Serena bubbled.

Relm looked back at Serena and the fifty dolphins behind her.

"I know of a great hunt," Relm called. "And we shall all be able to feed for many Blacks and Lights. But you must follow me, because only I have the knowledge of this Epic."

Serena laughed. Pryor was behind them and laughed too.

She cried out, "Go on then Matriarch Relm. Show us the way!"

Relm, suddenly aware that Pryor was watching, became very shy and retreated behind her. Pryor bubbled and took up the lead again. Serena and Relm returned to Relm's nursery group and met up with Ridge. The girls swam together and sang songs. Neo regularly played with them too, although he wasn't always welcome.

"Go play with the boys, Neo. Make some alliances, go fight them," Ridge often told Neo.

"Look, I need to grow a little older first."

"You are six cycles, Neo. And you already left your own nursery family."

"Well I didn't exactly leave on my own."

"What do mean, Neo?" asked Serena.

"I was made to leave. The females were going to have calves soon and my mother died so she wasn't there to…"

Serena did not want to hear any more. She hadn't told them about her mother yet, and she wasn't sure that she would. Serena swam away for a moment trying to clear her thoughts. She remembered what Anu had said. Had her mother really been taken by the slowspeakers? What did they want her for? Food, of course. They were predators. Or had she invaded their territory by going onto the beach? Serena had questions, but because there were no answers she had to put the questions away until later. Her attention turned back to Neo who had obviously lost his mother and was forced to leave the nursery too early. He needed more practice fighting before attempting to form alliances with other males. He had to become more mature before the males would accept him. Serena sounded the signal for a chase, two pops like a double door knock. Neo squeaked and took off with Serena, Ridge, and Relm close behind.

By now the dolphins' migration had taken them from the northern waters of Mexico to the lower coast of Central America. The water was much warmer than Serena was used to and she worried that she had traveled too far. She thought that certainly Alatina would not have come this far south into warm waters. The dolphins were at the surface regularly allowing the air to cool the blood in their dorsal fins, which would help cool their entire bodies. One of the schools' matriarchs was singing a piece of an Epic, recanting a song from her own mother of when she discovered the knowledge of the Great River that flows through the sea.

Serena had heard this Epic song before. The Great River was used by thousands of traveling creatures where the current is steady and fast. Serena looked down and cast upon an enormous herd of very large yellow fish schooling below them.

"Hey, Ridge, Relm, look at the big fish following us."

"Yeah, these are scavenger fish." Ridge explained. "They're waiting for us to hunt and then they clean up the leftovers."

The fish were too big to be considered a food source so Pryor sent more scouts to look for an easier hunt that morning. The rest of the company cruised around waiting for the scouts to return. Serena was growing restless.

"This is as boring as watching coral grow." Serena bubbled. "There must be something we can do. Come on," she whistled at Relm, "Let's follow the scouts. We can help them."

"I don't know, Serena. The matriarch Pryor ordered everyone to stay close."

"I'm too warm, lets get out to the open sea for a while and cool off. We'll certainly find food out there, and maybe a little fun."

"I'm with you," chirped Neo. "I'll follow you anywhere, Serena." He blew bubbles flirtatiously.

"Ok, that's one," whistled Serena ignoring Neo's bubbles.

"Ridge, you in for the hunt or not?"

"I'm ready to hunt anytime, anywhere, Serena," she proved with a swipe of her tail.

Relm still looked reluctant.

"What will Pryor say when we get back? She'll rake us all for sure. What if the scouts come back and we miss out on the meal?"

"We're going to catch up with the scouts and help them," urged Neo.

"Six casts are better than two," chirped Ridge.

"If we hurry we'll catch up. Let's move!"

Serena took the lead and saw Relm look back towards her mother before deciding to follow. The four young dolphins bolted away from the company and when they were beyond the range of echolocation, they changed course in pursuit of Pryor's scouts. The water was a little cooler away from shore but still quite warm. This area was mostly sandy with a few rocky outcroppings here and there. The fish communities congregated around the rocks for protection. The colors were not as bright here as they were at home. There didn't seem to be as many fish. It suddenly occurred to Serena that she hadn't seen a shark in several Lights. Maybe sharks didn't live in this part of the sea. Maybe because the water was so warm. She told the other three dolphins what she was thinking and the others agreed that it was unusual.

"You'd think," chirped Relm, "that with all the slowspeakers around with food the sharks would be everywhere."

"True but maybe the slowspeaker hunters drove them away from their kill and out of their territory," guessed Ridge.

"Perhaps," Neo pondered, "the slowspeaker hunters hunt the sharks."

The girls blew bubbles at him.

"What would they want with a shark? To eat it?"

"Yuck! With that tough skin!"

Serena was silent. She knew slowspeakers were different then they were. They took her mother, why wouldn't they take a shark?

"Maybe slowspeakers eat lots of different foods. More than fish and shrimp. Maybe they eat large prey, as killer whales do," chirped Serena quietly.

"Have you seen a slowspeaker up close?" asked Relm. "I have, and their teeth are not for ripping their food. Their teeth are flat and shiny. There is no way they could tear shark skin with their flat teeth."

"When did you see a slowspeaker that close?" Neo asked.

"Well, mother took me to see some, a little one and a big one, on a small skywhale. We looked at them and they looked at us. The big one reached out for us, but I didn't want to be touched. I was afraid. They opened their mouths and showed us their teeth. I though at first they were jawing at me, but mother said that the slowspeakers open their mouths to greet, not to fight. Strange, huh?"

Serena could tell that Relm felt proud of the knowledge she had of slowspeakers.

"I like the slowspeakers," squeaked Ridge. "They give us food, let us ride their skywhales, and they hunt sharks."

Serena whipped around, "Ridge, we have not seen slowspeakers eat sharks. We don't know."

"Sorry, Serena. You're right, we haven't seen it."

The four dolphins continued casting and swimming when finally the young dolphins cast upon the scouts swimming towards them.

"What are you doing here?" demanded the scouts. "Where is the rest of the school?"

"We came to find you. We wanted to help you." Serena squeaked.

The two older scouts were not amused with them.

"Come with us. We're going back to the school. We have found another slowspeaker skywhale with food. They saw us and they are following us."

Ridge blew bubbles, "I knew the slowspeakers were good, they are coming to feed us. They share their hunt. Like we do with each other."

Serena spy hopped out of the water and saw a large skywhale in the distance rumbling noisily towards them. She did not trust the slowspeakers that much. Hadn't they scared them away and taken back the shrimp? Serena told this to Neo who chuffed.

"Serena, the slowspeakers are not going to hurt us. They helped us. Come on, let's get back to the school with the good news."

The four young dolphins and the two scouts sped back towards the large school. Serena did not feel right about the skywhale headed their way. Why would they follow them to share their catch? Serena was a problem solver, not a mind reader, so she didn't dwell in her thoughts on the motivations of the slowspeakers. She simply followed the scouts and trusted that her matriarch knew what was for the best. The scouts reported back the news of the ship. Pryor was very excited about the easy meal for the party. However, descent from the other matriarchs immediately challenged Pryor.

"I will not allow my school to be beggars from slowspeakers. We will not have our food delivered to us."

"It doesn't matter where the food comes from, as long as it comes."

"We can not know they are on their way to feed us."

"We must leave and hunt elsewhere, I do not like being followed by a sky-whale. I will not wait for it."

Matriarch Pryor took these ideas into consideration and decided, "If the skywhale comes and does not give food, than we will leave and go hunt together as a group."

The matriarch Tonina gave a shrill cry and swiped her tail at matriarch Pryor for control. Pryor fought back hard once again winning the dominance fight.

"My school is leaving!" screamed Tonina. "Come!"

Relm and Ridge immediately obeyed and following their mothers and the rest of their nursery.

"Wait!" cried Serena. "You're leaving? When a meal is so close? What will you do without the company?"

"Sorry, Serena. I trust matriarch Tonina more than Pryor," chirped Ridge.

"Come with us, Serena," whistled Relm. "We'll hunt together."

Serena had a choice to make. One of many choices. Dolphins had the advantage of free will, deciding their fate and serving the consequences for choices and actions. She turned to Neo who, like herself, was a loner. Would she be safer in the main herd? Would she find her family if she joined the smaller one? Would she be better off with friends? Her decision came with realization that friends were the most important things in life. Most of a dolphin's life is spent building and maintaining strong relationships. She decided to join her friends. She then turned to Neo.

"Neo…I'm going with them."

Serena felt some sadness at the thought of leaving him behind. He would not be allowed to join the nursery group. He would have travel on his own.

Neo chuffed in disappointment and suddenly swam away to join up with the other dolphins in their swimming pattern. Serena joined the smaller formation. As the small nursery school started to swim away, the rumble of the skywhale was suddenly now upon them. The skywhale was not headed straight towards them. It was headed off to the side as if it would go right by. It seemed to be slowly circling them.

Serena did not feel right about the situation and swam over Tonina whistling, "Matriarch Tonina, I feel an unfamiliar presence in the water. We should go now. Away from the skywhale."

Serena heard splashes in the water, as if a dolphin was performing circular plop jumps to keep a fish school tightly circled. The slowspeakers were dropping something into the water around them. The skywhale was coming around behind them when the warning whistle pierced the water.

"Flee! Now! Away!"

The screams came from Pryor who led the large school toward Serena and her group. Tonina turned and raced away, followed by her group. At top speed Tonina raced ahead to show her nursery group to safety when suddenly she was stopped. As if she had crashed into an invisible wall Tonina was stopped in the water. Serena cast all around Tonina to check if she was hurt and find out what made her stop. Serena was puzzled. Tonina had run directly into a fine web, like the shrimp had been in. It was a network of strands that had no discernable pattern, making the netting hard to cast and almost impossible to see.

Dolphins surrounded Tonina as she regained herself and headed to the surface to breathe. As she turned around Tonina's tail became tangled in the net. She struggled and twisted getting more caught. Screams were filling the water from every direction. Serena turned one of her eyes behind her to see dolphins panicked, jerkily swimming in all directions. All formations had been broken. A dolphin screamed from beyond vision.

"Pryor is caught!"

Serena turned both eyes back on Tonina watching her becoming increasingly tangled as her wide eyes showed panic beyond reasoning. Pryor screamed to the others from somewhere below.

"To the surface everyone! Stay away from the Tangler!!"

Relm's mother tore and bit at the net but it was harder than any grass or coral. It would not break. She gave out a cry, and Serena knew that Relm's mother had been a friend to Tonina for many years, but freeing her was hopeless. She rubbed Tonina's pectoral flipper one last time and took off for the surface to breathe.

"Relm!" she cried. "Stay with me!"

Serena, Ridge, and Relm followed her. They sucked in a breath and Serena spy hopped at the surface. Dolphins were jumping in fear all around her. The screams of fifty dolphins were deafening in the water.

The skywhale was now stopped. This skywhale had a long, high tower with the Tangler attached. The Tangler appeared to be a circle, and just as the dolphins circle up their prey and bring them to the surface, the Tangler was doing the same thing to the dolphins. Serena dove back down hoping to escape out the bottom. She pushed through dolphins and fish trying to find the way out. But the Tangler was surrounding them from below; the only opening was at the surface.

"Serena!!" Neo darted by her and turned back around with a flip of his tail.

"The dolphins," Neo screeched, "Many are caught at the bottom. They can't get free!"

"Follow me!" Serena cried, darting for the surface.

She cast and found that where she had just breathed the netting was covering the surface!

"No," she softly squeaked. Serena smashed her body into the net, but it wouldn't move.

"We must find an opening!"

Serena and Neo passed dozens of dolphins wrapped and drowning in the Tangler. Dolphins were pushing helplessly upwards on the net trying to get a breath. Serena closed her eyes and cast around her. Two dolphins in the net were already dead. The net was engulfing the school. Serena knew that the Tangler would completely surround them if she didn't hurry. Finally there was a hole. It was only half a dolphin length wide. Serena tried to scream above the horrible deafening sound of dolphins dying and fearing their deaths.

"Follow me! There is an opening! Follow me!" Serena nudged Neo hard in the side.

"Go ahead of me. Jump through and stay at the surface until you are past the danger."

Neo hesitated. "I don't want to jump up when I don't know what's on the other side."

"Death is on this side, Neo! Go now!" Serena barked.

Neo swam upward and he was gone. Serena zipped back downward, away from the closing trap screaming at the others to follow her. A few dolphins joined her formation. Ridge and Relm appeared together out of a tangle of dolphin bodies.

"I can't find my mother!" Relm cried.

"Follow me, I know the way out. Listen, we must go one at a time or we'll all die!"

Serena forced her way to the surface and the opening in the net that was getting smaller every second.

"Go now! Relm, Ridge jump out!"

Relm, Ridge, and then Serena jumped one at a time right at each other's tails through the small opening. Serena landed with a belly flop and tried not to move too much or she would be caught in the net below her. More dolphins got out behind her but the panicking dolphins rushed the opening making it impossible for anyone else to escape. Serena, Ridge, and Relm made it to the end of the net and shot out like rockets for the open sea. Other dolphins that escaped kept on going but Serena stopped and turned around. She wished she hadn't.

The skywhale was pulling the Tangler out of the water. Dolphins ensnared were pulled out of the water able to finally breathe only to have their own weight break their bones as they fell through the net. Dead dolphins were lifted up onto the skywhale. Serena watched in horror as one dolphin, hooked to the net by her beak, was being pulled high into the air while she thrashed, breaking her jaw but still unable to escape. A huge wheel at the top of the tower was pulling the net. The dolphin was pulled through the crushing wheel and fell fifty feet onto the deck. When finally the Tangler was fully out of the water the slowspeakers rushed around dumping the dead dolphins back into the sea. They kept the other animals. The large yellow fish that had been in the shadow of the dolphins were all collected. It was a tuna fishing boat. Serena realized the yellow fish were what the slowspeakers wanted. Once the dolphins were all thrown back into the sea the skywhale rumbled away leaving death, blood, and abandoned dolphins.

Chaos reigned.

Relm and Ridge raced toward the sinking and floating dolphin bodies, screaming their mothers' names. Neo joined up with Serena, who floated motionless, in disbelief. Some of the dolphins who were thrown out of the net were alive, but could not swim. Their skin was ripped deep from the course netting, their minds unclear from the lack of oxygen. Blood clouded the water and forty dolphins were sinking into the dark waters below.

Serena echolocated into the gruesome scene to find Ridge and Relm. She pictured two moving dolphins pushing one that was not moving. It was Tonina, their matriarch. Her tail flukes were torn off and she had no heartbeat. The calf inside her was still. Ridge and Relm pushed her up to the surface but Tonina did not breathe. They continued pushing dolphins to the surface but they were soon overcome with exhaustion and grief. Suddenly Serena heard a sound from below that sent her heart racing. Bones crunching and skin tearing. Attracted by the smell of blood, sharks had appeared. They feasted on the enormous amount of food slowly falling towards them. They must have been following the skywhale to have appeared so fast. The sharks had known this was going to happen. Serena felt sick at the thought of it.

"Sharks!" cried Serena. "Fly!! Swim! Quickly away!"

Serena led Ridge, Relm, and Neo far from the encounter, out west towards the setting sun and the open ocean.

CHAPTER 4

The Journey Begins

The four dolphins swam wildly until they became exhausted. They did not know what to do or where to go. They rested their minds and bodies by floating still at the surface until nightfall. Serena tried not to let the images of the day enter her thoughts. Instead she imagined her nursery family, and life in the cool waters of her home range. The dolphins did not vocalize. For days they drifted in silence grabbing food as it came available, yet taking no joy in hunting. Relm cried out her mother's name as if she might appear out the blue.

Ridge was attacking anything she could find. She had found a sea cucumber and was displacing her anger by throwing it into the air and thrashing it against the water's surface. She carried the invertebrate creature miles on her pectoral flipper until she found a large rock to smash it on. After three days of mourning and swimming without purpose or direction, Neo attempted to brighten Serena's mood by bringing her a strand of seaweed for tag, but Serena was not interested. By now the ocean was so deep the dolphins could not cast the bottom. They were lost and alone.

Finally Neo chirped up, "Where are we going, Serena? We won't survive if we continue to drift."

Ridge and Relm clicked in agreement and looked to Serena for an answer. They were obviously hungry. Serena did not answer immediately. She had been thinking. For three days she had kept silent, but her mind was fully awake. Many memories passed through her mind; images of her mother and Alatina, wise and strong; Anu revealing that her mother was taken away by slowspeakers; the slowspeaker who scared the herd away from the shrimp; the slowspeakers who pulled the Tangler around them. She thought of Pryor and how her lack of knowledge put all the dolphins in peril. She thought of Alatina, who sang songs of the Epic, of her own adventures, and adventures of those who sang before her. Serena wanted new knowledge added to the Epic. Knowledge of the slowspeakers. She would not return to BrightWater without this knowledge. Serena whistled to the others, slow and deliberate.

"I am going to the Great River to discover the Epic song of the slowspeakers. I am going to go as far as I have to and find the meaning of our relationship in Nature with them. I don't understand them. They are like the ballooning spine fish that look innocent until you get too close, and then they blow out showing their hidden power. Never in any Epic have I heard of a horror that we just experienced. I can't just let it go. I won't ever let something like that happen again. I will pass on this knowledge as far as I can swim, and return only with a new Epic. The Nature of Slowspeakers."

Serena turned to face southwest and swam purposefully forward. The other dolphins buzzed in awe and amazement at Serena's sudden change in mood.

"Wait, Serena!" Neo whistled, "I coming with you!"

Ridge and Relm clicked at each other. They really had nowhere else to go, no school, and no knowledge of how to get back to nursery waters. They followed.

The dolphins were three hundred miles west off the coast of southern Mexico. They now hunted in earnest. Most of the time they swam in silence or sang songs to pass the time. Serena led the way southwest, navigating using her knowledge of currents and using first Light to confirm her direction. Dolphins were very good at sensing direction. Not only did they use the consistent Sun for help, they also relied on the magnetic poles of the Earth. Serena clicked Neo fully awake and he popped his head above the ocean's surface.

"First Light, Neo. Look how the sky changes colors with the rising of the light."

The pink and red hues reflected over the water, the glassy surface broken only by the two dolphin faces blinking in the sunlight.

Ridge was already scouting ahead casting for a school of fish. Neo was in a playful mood as usual and grabbed what he thought was a jellyfish he could wrestle. He immediately spit it back out.

"Whoa, Serena, mouth this thing, its not alive!"

Serena stole the jellyfish but spit it out straight away. It was hard, yet floated lazily around. It was clear, but tasted terrible. Serena jaw popped at it and looked curiously at it. What was it? Not food. She touched it with her flipper. Not alive. Relm swam over to see what was so interesting.

"Oh, I've seen those before. They gather around the skywhales. Slowspeakers don't even notice them, though."

Serena blew harsh bubbles at the mention of slowspeakers and swam away from the clear floating thing. Neo continued to play with the clear plastic bag that had probably been tossed off the side of a cruise ship. Serena cast for Ridge who was swimming back towards them. Her whistles were clear even though she couldn't yet be seen.

"Loads of fish ahead, all traveling one direction, I think we've reached the Great River."

The Great River was the south equatorial current of the Pacific, a constantly flowing river in the ocean that runs from northern South America across the ocean. The Great River was very wide and the northern part flowed in two directions like a highway, eastward and westward. Millions of animals used the equatorial currents to migrate across the Pacific and back again. Serena found swimming much easier now as she glided along in the current. The four dolphins had no trouble rounding up groups of silvery fish to swallow up whole. In this vast blueness Serena was constantly echolocating for whatever may be up ahead. She kept listening for the low rumbles of a skywhale.

The Black approached yet again in the never ending cycle of light and dark. Neo paired with Serena, buzzing her gently with rapid casting clicks. Serena had just let half of her mind disappear into unconsciousness when she saw a bright green light envelope her. Quickly coming back to full consciousness, she stopped in midwater and sat very still until the light went away. She cast in front of her and suddenly a trail of green haze lit up before her. Serena was startled but amazed at the bright lights in the dark. She twirled several times and watched the water erupt with light all around her. She whistled for Neo who appeared in a swirl of light.

"I know what this is!" clicked Neo excitedly.

"What?" squeaked Serena, as her bubbles produced more green trails.

"These are tiny animals, millions of them, who light up when they're bothered. They rise to the surface at night from deep waters. Watch this!"

Showing off like a clown, Neo jetted upward to the surface leaving a trail of green light behind him. He rocketed out of the black water in a spray of light. He turned on his side in midair and crashed back down causing a blast of light to radiate outward. From below, Serena watched in awe the natural beauty of the growing circle of light, like rings around a drop of water. Neo swam in tight circles at the surface trying to stir up the creatures whose lights had gone out. A short distance away Serena saw a haze of green growing closer and closer.

"Hey, Serena! This is cool!"

Ridge and Relm were now in on the fun. They beat their tails to make waves of light. Neo continued leaping, crashing, and spinning while Serena clapped her jaws open and closed, filling her mouth with bright shimmering light. The bioluminescent creatures entertained the dolphins for hours, until Serena finally decided she really needed to rest. Neo stayed alert first and took turns with the others keeping watch throughout the night. As they rested the current took the dolphins miles away from the bioluminescent ball.

The next several days Serena noticed that there were no birds in the sky. They were too far away from the shore. With the lack of predators from above, fish herded near the surface, unaware that a small school of hungry dolphins were casting them nearby.

After their meal Serena, Neo, Relm, and Ridge were about to start a game of tag when they became aware of a group of dolphins headed their way.

"Serena," Ridge warned, "These are open ocean dolphins. They're bigger than dolphins that live by the shore. They almost never visit the coast. They survive out here by deep diving to catch squid and fish."

Neo cast furiously towards the dolphins, "There are six of them, all males. It's a bachelor clan, Serena." He twitched nervously. Serena had never seen him so frightened, even during the tangler attack. Serena became alarmed. Bachelor clans are very dangerous because male dolphins can be very aggressive.

The six males surrounded the four young dolphins, circling them menacingly.

"What are you young calves doing out here?" whistled one.

"We are not calves!" barked Neo.

"Really? Where is your alliance then?"

Neo remained silent. It was very clear that he was frightened.

"Serena," Relm quietly chirped, "Let's get out of here."

"Leave us alone," Serena demanded of the rogue males.

This only seemed to provoke them. The males postured aggressively. Ridge popped her jaw in warning as one male approached her.

"Oh, feisty little shore dolphin," whistled the largest one. "Think you can fight us?"

Two males attacked Ridge at once, raking their teeth along her back. An explosion of dolphin fighting erupted as Ridge smashed her tail into the face of one of the males. Serena swam rapidly in tight circles to ward off the advances of an alliance of three males who were racing after her. Relm repeatedly leaped out of the water to escape. The noise was deafening as all ten dolphins buzzed, clicked, jaw popped, and squealed.

Neo was getting the worst beating. The older males displayed their dominance and raked him with their teeth. They repeatedly rammed him with their hard bony jaws. They continuously swam in front of Neo, trying to fluke him in the face. One good hit could have broken Neo's jaw, but Neo was fast and he evaded their powerful fluke thrusts each time. Serena flashed by him with three males on her tail. Neo zipped away after the males pursuing Serena. He grabbed one of the males by the tail and tore of chunk of skin out with his own set of sharp teeth. The males all left the girls and ganged up on Neo. Serena was afraid they might kill him so she swam up through the middle of the gang and tail slapped the largest male right in face. She whistled to Neo, Relm, and Ridge.

"Fly, Fly! Fast Away!"

Serena and Relm with Ridge and Neo right behind blasted across the water, porpoising with long, low leaps to move faster through the air. The gang of males took up the chase, however, clicking in delight at their new game. The chase might have gone badly for the young dolphins, but it was suddenly ended by the arrival of a huge skywhale. The six males immediately forgot their pursuit and raced over to the ship's bow. Serena heard them call it a Pusher as the marauding males dove into the bow wave. They whistled excitedly as they surfed in the surge of water pushed by the large cruise ship. Serena chuffed as the ship disappeared along with the dolphin bullies.

Neo was shaken. He was breathing rapidly and Serena bubbled her concern, "Are you alright, Neo?"

"I've had encounters like this before," Neo confessed. "The other male groups always just attack me. I went back to my nursery, but they attacked me too. I just don't fit in anywhere."

"You fit in with us, Neo," Serena cooed.

"That's right," Relm chirped. "We're our own dolphin herd now."

The dolphins swam in silence for a while, following the trail of the skywhale. They came across all kinds of slowspeaker debris, often found in coastal waters by dolphins. There were hard clear substances, in many shapes and sizes, and food garbage that attracted hundreds of hungry fish. The dolphins caught them readily. Relm complained that her eyes were hurting. Although diluted, an inky brown substance that tasted terrible was flowing in the wake of the ship.

"Ouch! What is it in the water?" Relm chirped.

"It must be coming from the skywhale." Serena figured.

"Whatever it is, let's get out of here." Relm insisted. The dolphins veered off as nightfall approached. Serena didn't know the ship was dumping excess oil and garbage into the sea. Just before Black, Serena saw a bird in the sky. She hoped that was a sign of shallow waters nearby.

Neo was not his usual playful self the next few days. His wounds were healing fast, but they were still painful. He made himself feel better by gloating to the girls how he had taken a chunk out of one of the male's tails. Relm and Ridge pretended to fight off more dolphins playfully slapping the water and biting at bubbles. After a week, the story they were telling would have convinced others that they had fought a pack of fifty big males and sent them porpoising. Serena wanted to find some shallows. She was tired of drifting out here in the never ending blue. She had no idea how big the open ocean was.

Serena had lost count of the days and nights they had traveled, but it had been over a month. They swam an average of five miles per hour moving them almost one hundred miles every single day. Serena closed her eyes and focused. She cast the sound waves of rapid clicks through her melon out into the deep blue. Nothing returned. She opened her eyes and became nervous. She had never been out this far. So far from her family, so far from the shallows, so far from everything. Where was she leading her friends? These young orphaned dolphins trusted her so completely.

Serena involuntarily blew a burst of bubbles out through her blowhole as she realized in surprise that she was the acting matriarch! She was the leader. The lives of her friends were under her responsibility. Serena looked around at her companions. Neo was acting like he didn't have a care in the world, carrying a strand of seaweed on his pectoral flipper that he must have picked up long ago. It had been days since they had seen any plant life.

Perhaps he felt like he was back with his nursery, surrounded by females, letting others plan the hunts, and following orders. He was trying to delay growing up. Eventually Neo would have to join a male group and fight for his dominance. He might become like one of the males that had attacked them. He would become part of an Alliance. The older males formed bonds as strong as the bonds between older females. Sometimes an alliance between males lasted for years and years.

Ridge looked resolute as if this journey was a test of her strength and wisdom. She was looking for adventure. She was alert, as if expecting trouble at any moment. Serena cast her; she was definitely the strongest dolphin among them. Ridge felt herself being cast and looked over at Serena. Serena whistled a greeting, as if checking up on her. They went back to swimming in silence. Serena glanced back at Relm. She seemed tense and nervous. Serena thought she probably had not stopped visualizing the Tangler attack. Serena hoped Relm would be able to make the journey. After all, she was only following Serena because she had no one else to follow. Serena cast forward again still receiving no echo in return.

The Pacific Ocean was big, very big, and very deep. The open ocean was like a desert, nothing to see but blue in every direction. The young dolphins were not used to seeing such an open void. It was scary because a predator could come from anywhere, even below. The dolphins were constantly echolocating looking for predators, but even more importantly, food. Serena had only eaten ten pounds in the past three days. She was hungry. So were Neo, Ridge, and Relm. Life was so scarce out here. They would come upon pockets of fish either too small or too big. But Serena was becoming less and less picky as each opportunity to feed swam into view.

"How much farther do we have to go before reaching shallow waters, Serena?" Relm gurgled. "My stomach hurts." Serena could see that Relm was weak. She was feeling the same way. It felt harder to swim, her muscles felt tight. Ridge and Neo did not waste any energy playing and fighting. Their muscles were hurting too.

"I wonder if I'd be able to hunt even if a school of sardines swam right into my face?" Ridge murmured.

The current helped move the dolphins along. Four days later they caught a small school of juvenile jacks. The fish felt so good going down Serena's throat she thought it might have been the best meal she'd ever had. But it wasn't enough. Relm was starving. Her skin looked sunk in where fatty blubber had once been. It had been two weeks since she had a good meal. Serena no longer echolocated and each side of her brain drifted in and out of consciousness; back and forth. The group slowed to the pace of the current. They hardly moved at all. Even Neo didn't make a noise. They floated at the surface; exhausted, hungry, lost. Serena remembered her little brother Seris and how he cried when he was stuck in the cave. A distress call. Three high pitched squeaks that swooped up in pitch. It was a call designed for long-distance travel. She knew no one would hear it. She knew no one was coming to their rescue. But she cried out anyway.

"Save, Save, Save!"

She called out all day and all night. She was too exhausted to echolocate. If a shark found them now Serena knew she would not have the strength to fight it off. And out here there were no beaches to escape to.

"Save, save, save."

The four dolphins floated together at the water's surface in the dark. They were completely blind now to any predators. They might be able to hear something but they would have no warning and no defense anyway. Relm barely had enough energy to breathe. Her slow, raspy breaths gave away her weakness. Her skin was burned and chapped from being exposed to the sun. Aside from Serena's calls no one spoke or made a sound. No one complained about the pain or the fear, and no one admitted to losing hope.

For Serena, the worse pain was in her heart. She felt responsible for her friends. She led them out into this ocean desert. She promised knowledge and adventure, and provided only torture and misery. Serena felt empty and numb. She felt her mind slipping down into emptiness. Her body silently slipped beneath the surface. She was falling, sinking, down into the depths of blackness and sorrow. Serena opened her eyes and saw only darkness. The surface was high above. Light began to escape her memory.

Serena awoke to find herself at the surface. Neo and Ridge were holding her up on their backs. She took at deep breath. Her lungs hurt; she had water in them. Serena chuffed, forcing water up and out of her blowhole. Once she was breathing easier she swam free of Neo and Ridge.

Ridge softly told Serena what happened, "We realized you fell underwater when the distress calls stopped. I don't know how we did it, Serena, but Neo and I dove and cast you deep underwater."

Neo continued, "We pushed you up and held you up on our backs. We were scared, Serena. I thought you had died. It seemed an eternity before you took a breath."

Serena buzzed her friends. She didn't know how to thank them. They had just saved her life.

She called out into the night, "Save, save, save!"

As if in answer to her call, the sun suddenly appeared over the horizon sending streaks of orange and pink gliding across the water. The dolphins blinked in the light as the sun rose higher to reveal a thin dark line in the distance.

It was land. Land! The water was becoming shallower and fish appeared out in droves. At first the dolphins did not react. They were so weak and groggy they didn't know if what they were seeing was real. Then Neo snapped his head to the side and showed off a big fish between his teeth before sucking it down. Ridge was next to begin hunting. She was moving so slowly that the fish didn't even register the danger until she clamped her jaws on a juicy white one. As the bottom became shallower Serena and Relm dove to the sand and slowly picked out fish hiding there. The dolphins ate all day long. Relm had regurgitated her fish at first. Her stomach muscles couldn't handle eating after so long, but she kept swallowing more fish and her body began to readjust. For the next week the dolphins slowly swam around the island, eating and getting their strength back.

CHAPTER 5

Flying Fish

The dolphins swam around the islands for days, exploring the rich diversity of life. Plant life became more abundant. Tasty and brightly colored fish were plentiful. Curious barracuda appeared and followed the dolphins for a while. The dolphins swam over a huge coral reef atoll, with bright, long coral circling a deep blue hole. A group of manta rays fluttered by like giant butterflies in slow motion. Serena and her dolphin party had reached the Tuamoto island chain, seventy-eight islands widely spread out along the South Pacific.

The young dolphins marveled at the beauty of this clear, warm water paradise. Several little cleaner fish rushed over to the dolphins and groomed them. By pecking off the micro plants and animals attached to the dolphins' skin, the dolphins get clean and the fish get dinner. Neo grabbed a piece of bright blue coral and broke it off the main stem; he swam proudly with it in his mouth and then threw it into the air with a quick whip of his head. He dashed after the coral piece, playing fetch with himself. Ridge was the first to notice the strange vessels headed in their direction.

They were kayaks, but Serena had never seen slowspeakers travel in anything so small before. The curious dolphins swam slowly over and inspected the long, small boats. Ridge even prodded one with her rostrum. The slowspeakers inside were very calm, not moving much at all. Serena liked that, she became more calm too. Neo came zooming by at just that moment and tossed his coral piece into the air. A slowspeaker caught it! All four dolphins looked like corks as they bobbed in the water, their heads sticking out. They stared at the slowspeaker. What was it going to do with Neo's coral?

"Hey, give it back!" Neo whistled.

The human in the kayak pulled back its arm and threw the coral as hard as it could. It splashed in the water not too far off. Neo blasted away, chasing after the coral like a fish on the run. He grabbed it and threw it around again.

"Do you think the creature understood Neo?" Relm asked as they ducked back beneath the water.

"No." Serena said with confidence. "They don't know our speech. Perhaps just the sound of Neo made it throw the coral back. Watch, I'll show you."

Serena surfaced again and clicked to the slowspeaker, "Hey, come swimming in here with us."

The slowspeakers didn't seem to even hear her. They continued paddling along. The dolphins kept pace.

"Give me that stick!" Ridge cried to the human.

It looked down at her but made no motion to give up the paddle. Even Relm got into the game.

"My name is Relm!" she whistled.

No answer.

"See, they can't even hear us, let alone understand us. They are just too slow."

Serena, bored with the game, swam off to join Neo. She stole his coral and a game of chase had begun.

After several hours of chasing each other around the atolls Ridge clicked, "I'm getting hungry, let's hunt."

The dolphins swam toward the nearest shoreline. They formed the hunting position they'd used many times; Serena and Ridge taking the lead with Relm and Neo behind. Relm and Neo cast around on either side and looked above the water for signs of fish. Serena and Ridge were ahead casting the shore. At exactly the same time their castings revealed hundreds of silvery mullet hanging out in the extreme shallows where the tide had washed in. Serena immediately chirped directions. She and Ridge would swim up either side of the fish and Relm and Neo would swim up the center trapping them in the shallow water into a tight little ball. Easy meal.

The plan worked, at first. But as the fish became cornered they did something very odd, surprising the young dolphins. They jumped! The fish leaped right out of the water and over the dolphins' heads. The shocked dolphins froze. The middle of their circle was empty and the fish were swimming away down the beach. Neo rushed after them trying to catch one, but Serena sharply whistled him back.

"What just happened?" squeaked Neo.

Relm was dumbfounded, "The fish have learned to fly."

"Don't be foolish, follow me." Serena turned tail and pushed herself back into deeper water. The dolphins regrouped and swam down the beach.

"I have an idea," chirped Serena. "Neo, you go about two lengths ahead of us and spiral around in the mud where the fish are concentrated. We'll wait back here and as the fish fly into the air to escape you, we will catch them. They will land right in our mouths!"

The dolphins giggled with excitement, bubbles streaming from their blowholes. This game was going to fun, if it worked. They waited for the mullet to calm down before swimming back into the shallow mudflats. The four dolphins crept up slowly. Serena motioned for Neo to go and he burst forward. Neo blew bubbles with joy as he splashed and stirred up the mud. He swam tight circles in the very shallow water. Just as before, the fish went flying into the air to escape the attack. But this time three massive jaws, each filled with almost a hundred teeth, cut off their escape. The girls floated with their heads above the surface and their mouths wide open. A mullet landed right in Serena's mouth. Before it even realized it was caught, the fish was crushed by the clamping of a hundred sharp teeth that fit perfectly together like a zipper. Serena flipped the fish head first with her tongue and swallowed it whole. She instantly opened her mouth again to catch another one. Neo even caught a few in the muddy shallows.

Once all the fish had stopped leaping, either because they had escaped or been swallowed, the dolphins moved down the beach and played their game again. This time it was Relm who started the jumping fish into their blind panic, causing them to leap haphazardly into the dolphins waiting jaws. They continued playing this hunting game all day until the tide began to go out, and all the animals were forced to leave the muddy flats.

For the next month the dolphins traveled west from island to island along the atolls. Food was plentiful and the days were long. The natural beauty of the ocean here made the dolphins feel comfortable and tranquil. Serena had never seen coral so bright in color. They were not the only dolphins to inhabit this precious piece of the Earth. The four young dolphins came across other dolphin groups who appeared to be local. Their home range spanned the atolls and they were not aggressive when Serena approached them. The other dolphins had grown up here; they had never been anywhere else. They thought the entire ocean was like this. They had no concept of the vast wide world. Serena had tried to tell the dolphins about the great dangers of slowspeaker nets but most didn't have any idea what she was talking about.

There were a few dolphins who came to speak with her away from the groups. These were really old dolphins, in their thirties, and they had experienced many trials in their lives. Serena listened to them hoping to gain knowledge.

"I have seen what you spoke of, but not for many cycles. Great Tanglers that took everyone with them. We remember those dark times where entire herds were killed. This occurred all over the Ocean, there was nowhere safe. But that was when I was a calf, and the slowspeakers seem very kind now. We are distressed to hear of it again."

Serena told them in more detail of what happened, and they nodded as they remembered similar things.

"I have never been that far south along the coast, but similar Tanglers used to be farther north as well."

Serena cried out to them, "Why have you never told anyone these things? Why do your schools not know of the dangers? Had you told others, our matriarch Pryor would have known to stay clear of the skywhale!"

Serena was upset that other dolphins had known about the trouble and did not pass on their knowledge.

"I have not encountered such a thing in over twenty cycles! After danger has passed, one forgets the pain it causes. We felt no need to warn against something we haven't seen for so long. Do not worry about it any longer. Stay here with us. You'll never see a Tangler again."

Serena tried to imagine living in this lovely, picturesque place her entire life. She thought about joining one of these nursery groups, settling in, having a calf, and remaining here in safety. But would she be content? Serena thought about this for days. The other dolphins seemed happy here. Neo was always playing and flirting with other dolphins. He had found a new game of causing as much trouble as he could for the poor sea urchins, who would spend all day climbing a rock only to be knocked down again with a swish of Neo's tail. He was never serious and always mischievous. Ridge and Relm seemed content. Relm especially. Serena had never seen her so active and involved. She was eating well and joining in on all the games. She was socializing more with the other dolphins. Serena realized one afternoon that Relm had been gone for several hours. When she returned Relm explained that she had been helping to watch some calves while the mothers were hunting.

"Relm," whistled Serena, "I didn't know you were so close with the other group. They actually let you watch their calves?"

"Yes, along with several other young girls. By the way, they want to meet you, Neo."

Neo blew out a burst of bubbles.

"Me? Why?"

"I told them you were not a threat and had no alliance yet. I told them how you fought the rogue males. They are curious about you."

If dolphins blushed Neo would have turned scarlet. Instead he swam a few barrel rolls.

"What do you think, Serena? Do you want to join them?"

All three dolphins turned to wait for Serena's answer. She realized what was happening. She was losing her group. They wanted to join another group to stay in these pristine waters. Serena had to admit that she too had debated staying. But now that she was faced with it, she knew her path. There was no decision to make.

"No, I will not join the nursery group. I will continue on until I discover the Epic song and finish the journey. I will return home."

The other three were stunned. Over the last month Serena hadn't even mentioned the Epic or the journey. They had all thought they would be staying here for a long time. Serena's mind was made up. She would go alone if she had to. The thought of traveling alone frightened her. She would be sad to leave them behind, but she had to go on. Serena turned and swam away from Neo, Ridge, and Relm. She headed southwest, towards the Great River, back towards the endless blue, and the unknown.

Serena told herself the others would be better off back there; a home range, a nursery, a family. Relm was smart to stay behind. She would be living without hunger, loneliness, or fear. But Serena would miss her softness and poetic songs. She would miss her trusting eyes. Relm had made her feel like a leader. Ridge, no doubt would spend her days playing in the large waves off the islands. Serena would miss her bravery. Ridge had shown Serena that strength was more a power of the mind than body. Serena now felt that she was leaving her strength of mind behind her.

Then she thought of Neo. She would miss his playfulness and positive outlook. He was an entertainer and an inventor. Anything could be turned into a toy, and anytime was a good time for a game. Serena remembered when Neo gave her the seaweed he'd been carrying for three days. She asked him why he was willing to give it up.

He had said to her, "A toy's usefulness dies with time, but friendship never dies. Time makes it valuable."

Serena stopped. Would she abandon their friendship so easily? Should she leave without at least trying to persuade them to follow? Serena turned around. She decided not to leave without them. They had begun this journey with her. This was not her journey, but theirs as well. Serena started to swim back. Unexpectedly, out of the blue, she heard her name being called. She cast ahead to see Neo rapidly swimming her way. Serena called back and in an instant they were reunited spiraling around each other.

Neo chuffed at her, "Don't ever do that again, Serena. I thought I'd lost you."

They swam together synchronized in rhythm with the waves above back toward the island chain.

"This journey is mine too, Serena. And you are my friend, my alliance. I go where you go. Besides," he added with a flip of his tail, "you'd die of boredom without me along."

Serena giggled and nudged Neo in the side. Just then Relm and Ridge appeared.

"Hey, we're coming too!"

"Didn't think you could have survived without me to protect you, did you?" Ridge squawked.

"I'm sorry, Serena. You know I'd never leave you. You know that I love you!" Relm rubbed her flipper along Serena's.

"Of course I know, and I love you too, all of you. And I'll never leave anyone behind again."

The four dolphins began the journey once more, porpoising in fast low leaps across the water. Serena saw more flat islands ahead, but knew that all too soon the open blue would be before them.

CHAPTER 6

Sharks and Sea Sponges

Five days out to sea the dolphins once again were not catching enough fish. Relm frantically scanned the waters for food. Food would come in uneven patterns, nothing for two days, and then suddenly they would be able to gorge themselves on a huge school. One morning after a good meal of silver fish the dolphins heard a low rumble in the distance.

"It's a skywhale!" clicked Relm.

Ridge whistled excitedly, "We could ride it to shore. Its a Pusher!"

Bubbles streamed from her blowhole. "I remember bow riding with my nursery. Remember, Relm? The thrill of riding the wave with the water rushing across your body, I can't wait." Serena was unsure that the skywhale would be safe. She didn't want to make the same mistake of trusting the slowspeakers only to be attacked.

She chuffed to stop Ridge from swimming around in excitement, and clicked to the others, "We will stay clear of the skywhale until we are certain it has no Tanglers. Then we will ride it until we either reach shore or we must eat."

Serena listened for the direction of the rumbling and swam out of its path. Ridge and Relm wanted to catch the ride head on, but they didn't want to fight Serena either so they swam along side of her. The enormous cruise ship came into view and passed by without incident.

Neo trilled, "It looks safe, Serena." He rubbed his pectoral flipper to hers. "Let's go for it."

Serena nodded. Ridge and Relm took off for the ship with Neo and Serena close behind. The dolphins leaped in front of the boat. Serena whistled as she felt a blast of water from behind push her forward. She had to close her eyes for a moment to adjust to the speeding water rushing on either side of her.

"Yeah!" cried Neo leaping up through the waves. "Now this is bow riding!"

The giant cruise ship pushed an enormous amount of water in front of it. It was like surfing a constant wave.

"Whoo!" Ridge squealed with delight as she let her muscles relax and rode the waves.

Serena turned on her side and looked up to see the small images of slowspeakers looking down at her, extending their long tendrils in her direction. She was glad they couldn't reach her from way up there. Every few hours she would look back up at them, they seemed to always be there looking down at her. Black came and the fast pace was starting to wear the dolphins down. They had never heard of other dolphins bow riding for so long. Serena knew that what they were doing was unusual for dolphins. They rode the waves for a few more hours then Serena squealed to the others that they had to leave the skywhale. She was exhausted and needed to rest. The others agreed and veered off watching the skywhale disappear into the darkness.

"I'll take the first watch Serena, you rest," clicked Neo.

She chirped back a thank you and floated motionless for a while allowing her mind to rest. Ridge and Relm floated nearby almost close enough to touch. In the dark the dolphins rested.

Dawn approached. Serena watched Neo as he was laying upside down right at the water's surface, looking at his own reflection. In the early morning light the angle was just right to see a blurry image. Neo pondered his freckles for a while, turning his head this way and that, before finally flipping over to breathe.

He looked at Serena and echolocated her. "Your stomach is empty. We need to hunt."

"The water is not so deep now," Serena observed.

"I can cast the bottom. We may be near shore waters. Let's go fishing."

Ridge and Relm were already casting in all directions for food. Neo popped his head above the water and saw a group of birds swirling in the distance.

"Flyers!" he trilled. "This way!"

And for the first time in his life, Neo led the hunt.

After many Lights and Blacks, the Great River changed direction. Instead of flowing west, now it was headed south. Ridge was correct when she thought the change meant that more shallow waters were not far. The dolphins were several hundred miles off the south-east coast of Australia. They had crossed the Pacific Ocean in four months. They left the South Equatorial current and entered the East Australian current. Serena led them between Australia and New Zealand, coming up on the southern tip of the Australian continent. The water here was very different from the island atolls. It was colder, murkier, and the waters were rough. The fish here were different. Most of the species Serena had never seen before. Even the sea bugs were different. The four stayed clear of any dolphin groups in the region. They swam close into shore to find food. There were boats everywhere, zooming around fast. Neo started chasing after one to ride in its wake, but Serena called him back. She was wary of the slows-peakers still, even though it had been a long time since the Tangler, and every slowspeaker they had come across from that time had not tried to harm them.

The dolphins swam off shore to keep out of the way of fast skywhales. They swam lazily around in the deeper waters taking the opportunity to relax and rest their minds. Serena could not rest, however. Something in the back of her mind was keeping her alert. She felt that something was not quite right. She felt eyes on her. She looked around and cast around her. Nothing.

"Neo," She called quietly. "Neo, I think that something is out there."

"What? Where?"

"I don't know, but I can feel it."

Neo suddenly turned and cast behind him, he thought he had seen a shadow out of the corner of his eye. Serena turned her head the other way. She thought a shadow had passed by that way too. Everything seemed strangely quiet. Suddenly, from below, a massive black shape rocketed upwards and rammed into Relm, knocking her out of the water in an explosion of spray. Serena spun around to see and cast an enormous shark, larger than she had ever seen. It was dark grey on top, but its belly was pure white. It was circling a stunned Relm, who was struggling to get to the surface for air. The great white shark was observing Relm with its lidless, emotionless black eyes. Serena watched as the shark's eyes rolled back white and knew it was going to finish Relm off.

Without a second to lose Serena screamed her highest, loudest scream possible and rammed the shark in the belly with as much force as she could muster. Ridge was right behind, jaw clapping and buzzing to find the most sensitive part of the shark. She went for the eyes. She slapped her tail hard against its eye, but the eye was rolled back white and little damage was done. However, it did have the effect of the shark keeping its eyes rolled back. The great white shark had rolled its eyes back to protect them while it attacked its prey, making it blind, but Serena knew the shark still sense Relm with sensors in its snout. The great white could also sense their movements by picking up on the vibrations in the water. The shark snapped its jaws just missing Ridge as she buzzed by. While the shark was still blinded, Neo raced to Relm and pushed her to the surface. She took a shallow, raspy breath.

"Neo," called Serena. "Get her out of here! Get her to shallow water."

Serena continued to bite and ram the shark as it slashed through the water. A rage had come over her. She wanted to kill this thing. This predator that may have killed her friend. She kept ramming the weakening shark until the skin on her lower jaw was shredded by the shark's rough, sand paper skin. Ridge dodged death yet again as she smashed her tail into the sensitive snout of the snapping shark. She continued to scream and jaw pop at it.

Finally, the shark realized its attempt had gone wrong and it bolted away into the depths to escape the counter attack. The dolphins swam fast to join Neo and Relm in their struggle to shore. If any humans had seen this spectacle they would have been mystified. Three dolphins swimming along the surface supporting a fourth, holding it up with their beaks, flippers, and even their backs. Relm was having trouble breathing. Serena cast Relm's body to look for damage. Her eyes opened wide. Inside Relm's body, blood was flowing to the point of impact; Relm had a wide gash in her side. It was painful for Relm to breathe so her breaths were slow and shallow.

Neo whistled to Relm, "Breathe, Relm. Open your eyes."

Serena knew if Relm fell fully unconscious she would die. Dolphins must be conscious, or at least semi-conscious, in order to breathe. Even if Relm was out of water she would suffocate if she lost consciousness. Relm buzzed and chirped a little. They needed to find a shallow bank to rest in. Ridge swam ahead to find a safe spot. Serena kept casting back, afraid the shark, or even other sharks, would sense Relm's distress and attack them again

Ridge came back with news of a shallow bank. It didn't seem occupied by slowspeakers or anything else. Neo pushed Relm into the shallows where she was able to rest in the sand. Serena cast Relm again. Her skin was badly torn, but there didn't seem to be any other damage inside Relm's body. Her heart rate slowed to normal. She breathed normally again. Neo, Ridge, and Serena floated close by whistling to Relm.

"How do you feel?" asked Serena.

Relm answered slowly in high-pitched chirps, "Side hurts. Breathing hurts."

"You have a large wound, but no damage internally, you'll be alright."

Ridge chirped up, "Just rest and then we can get some food."

Relm gurgled, "You should just leave me here and go on."

"Don't be silly Relm. I said I would never leave anyone behind. Either we all go, or no one goes."

Relm looked gratefully at Serena, "Thank you, Serena. Knowing I won't be abandoned is a great help to me." Relm began to softly cry. No tears came from her eyes. She only softly tweeted in a mournful way. Serena knew how she felt. Relm was crying over the loss of her mother. The pain was worse than any physical wound.

After a few hours of resting her mind and body, Relm was ready to continue on. Relm did not complain about the pain. Neo and Ridge flanked either side of Relm, while Serena searched for food. Dolphins tend to heal quickly. After several days the wound began to scar. The abrasion was a deep cut, however, and Relm was likely to carry a scar for the rest of her life. Relm had difficulty catching food, although the other dolphins rounded the fish up and let Relm partake of their catch.

Relm tried to keep her distance in the first few days. Serena knew Relm was feeling sorry for being a non-functional member of the group. Neo tried to cheer her up by buzzing her and bringing her interesting gifts, like sea sponges and sea stars. Serena spent most of her time spyhopping for skywhales. She wanted to see some slowspeakers and observe them. After the incident with the shark she felt braver. She no longer felt afraid of them, but wanted to know more about them. She spotted a boat in the distance and tail slapped the water to get everyone's attention.

"Ridge, Neo, follow me. We're going to check out those slowspeakers. Relm, you signal us if anything strange happens."

"Like what, Serena?"

"Anything you feel is out of the ordinary. Just keep watch."

Relm watched as her friends disappeared into the blue. Serena felt Relm casting her all the way to the skywhale. Serena looked out of the water and saw them. Slowspeakers! They were dangling their long legs off the edge of the skywhale. Serena swam closer. A slowspeaker tossed something down at her! Relm immediately leaped out of the water and smacked back down with a loud slap. Serena, Ridge, and Neo rushed back to her.

"The slowspeaker was throwing something at you with its long arms, Serena. I didn't know what it was!"

Serena opened her mouth to show them a piece of celery. Only the dolphins didn't know it was celery.

"Its crunchy, must be a plant of some kind."

Serena passed it to Neo.

"Doesn't taste like anything I've ever tasted."

Neo passed it to Ridge. She bit down on it a few times.

"Definitely plant. Why did it give this to you?"

Ridge passed it to Relm.

"Strange. You don't suppose it thought you would eat this?"

"Who cares!" whistled Neo grabbing the celery stalk. "We've got a new toy! It floats too!"

Neo tossed the celery into the air and chased after it.

"Maybe if we go back, they'll give us more things." Ridge said.

"Maybe," clicked Serena, "We'll find out tomorrow. Black is coming and I want to rest."

Serena let her mind go, she kept one eye opened and could hear, but did not echolocate and did not think about things. She rested.

"Neo!" whistled Ridge.

Neo heard his signature whistle and turned about.

"Serena's going visual, you might want to rest too. I have a feeling we'll be traveling come first Light."

She was right. As the Sun appeared on the horizon the next morning, Serena had already scouted out a morning feast. The dolphins spent the morning loitering around the shallow bays. Neo spent two lazy hours absently following an octopus, until it caught on it was being followed and angrily swam off in cloud of black ink. The green water was not as warm as the waters of the South Pacific islands but it was comfortable. The water was bright and the dolphins were able to see a good distance into the water.

When a slowspeaker boat cruised into the area, Relm hung back while the others approached the small vessel. Serena, Neo, and Ridge floated close to the bow and waited for the slowspeakers to look down at them. But this time they didn't come to look. Serena was suddenly aware of three bodies in the water. She heard a loud slap in the distance. She knew it was Relm's warning of something strange happening. Neo and Ridge raced off to Relm. Serena stayed behind.

Neo zipped back to Serena chirping, "Hey, Serena! Come on!"

"I'm going to stay. I'll be alright."

"Well, I'm going to stay too. Just be careful." Neo swam along her.

Serena took a breath and dove underwater. She knew the slowspeakers were in the water.

She was curious about them, but she approached apprehensively. Then she saw them. Serena had never seen them swimming before.

Neo laughed, "They looked like dead sea lions just floating on the surface. What are they doing?"

"Maybe they are just pretending." Serena chirped. "Be aware, they could move at any moment."

Serena carefully swam under the smallest of them and cast her first echolocation of humans. Information flooded her mind as she received images of the human bodies. The large heart, similar in size to her own. Internal organs, different; bony arms and legs, hands that looked like short flipper bones, brains. All these images entered her mind as the sound waves returned. She briefly thought about their lack of blubber and how her brain was larger than theirs.

Serena kept her distance but the slowspeakers were hardly moving at all. They were simply floating and looking around. She heard Relm's high whistles beyond sight and chirped back that she was safe.

Feeling a little braver, Serena swam closer to the creatures to get a better look. Neo stayed low looking up at them. Serena approached the smallest one, a female. The little girl's large eyes grew even wider as Serena approached. Serena wondered if that was a threat, but somehow she didn't think so. As Serena got closer the little girl let out a cry of amazement and bubbles streamed from her mouth. Serena blew bubbles back. Serena whistled a hello, but quickly realized that the slowspeaker couldn't possibly understand. Serena spun and zipped around the little girl trying to get her to follow. But the girl just floated there, watching. Serena paused. She was confused. How could this slow creature be dangerous? She seemed as harmless as floating seaweed. Serena felt a mutual curiosity between herself and the child.

Serena whistled down to Neo, "I think we're safe, Neo. I don't think the slowspeakers are very good swimmers. They must have to stay on the surface."

Neo tentatively swam over to one. "Hello, slowspeaker. Are you alive?" The slowspeaker suddenly moved its hand rapidly back and forth towards him, and Neo squeaked in fright, diving back down to the bottom.

Serena watched Neo dive and then looked back at the little girl. The girl's large eyes blinked from behind her mask. Serena liked the high squeaks the girl made now and again. It reminded her of a new born calf muttering nonsense and only squeaking for the fun of it. Serena decided the child was not dangerous. She knew she was ten times more powerful. Serena was not afraid. And she learned something very important to include in her Epic. Slowspeakers are weak in the water.

Neo returned with Ridge right behind. Relm stayed back. Neo and Ridge blew bubbles at the humans. Neo was brave again and inspected them for more celery. Ridge was bored within a few minutes.

"How can such a deadly hunter be so lethargic?"

Serena was still fascinated by the child. "This little slowspeaker seems as sweet as a baby dolphin. But I don't think they can swim very well."

Neo swam up beside Serena to look at the girl. The child's eyes blinked in innocent curiosity. Serena did not fear her, if fact a strange feeling was developing within her heart.

"I pity this poor creature, Neo. It can not control its own body enough to do anything but float helpless at the surface. This little creature might one day be like the other slowspeakers, dangerous predators."

"To bad we can't talk to her," Neo chirped. "Then we could ask her why they hurt dolphins. We could get her to stop using tanglers."

"Well, slowspeakers can not understand us. All we can do is learn how to stay out of their way."

Serena turned away resulting in the child squeaking a little. Serena wanted to tell her not to float around like a dead seal or something dangerous would see her from below, but she knew it was useless. Neo and Serena left the slowspeakers behind and Neo expressed openly what Serena had earlier been thinking about the slowspeakers.

"Maybe the slowspeakers in these waters are not hunters of dolphin. They seem here to be defenseless and powerless."

"Maybe only in the water they are weak," Serena pondered. "Maybe only the human calves are harmless."

"Look, we have traveled a long way, Serena. Maybe we've found the place we were looking for."

Serena paused confused.

"The place we've been looking for? What do you mean?"

Neo chirped, "You know, traveling all this way to find a peaceful spot, where dolphins can live without the slowspeakers affecting us. We don't have to be afraid of them here."

"Is that what you think we've been doing all this time. Looking for a new home?"

"Of course, what else have we come all this way for?"

Serena swam in silence thinking. What have they come all this way for? What was it she was looking for? An Epic. To sing about slowspeakers. To sing about her travels. To become wise. To be like Alatina. To be like her mother.

Maybe she had come all this way to find a new home. It sounded like a good idea.

Neo wouldn't have traveled this far for a mere story. He was looking for something more real. Something more present. Yes, Serena decided, we have come to find this place, where dolphins can live without the interference of slowspeakers. She only hoped the rest of her nursery group in BrightWater were safe, and felt a momentary pang of guilt for leaving them behind. She thought often of her nursery group, and about Seris. She wondered if he was doing alright.

Serena decided to continue along the shoreline in search of better hunting grounds. The dolphins traveled for weeks northwest along the coast. The water warmed up as they rounded to the west coast of Australia into the Indian Ocean. Food became more plentiful and, as the weeks passed, Serena saw creatures she had never seen before.

"Serena!" called Ridge. She had just returned from scouting. "You have to come look. These are the most bizarre things I've ever seen!"

Neo was especially interested after hearing an introduction like that. The dolphins followed Ridge and came across creatures that looked like big chunks of rock floating at the surface. They were dugongs, but Neo called them Lumps. Relm followed the group of dugongs for several hours. Their huge, gray bodies, slow movements, and playful nature fascinated her. They had short faces, tiny gray eyes, and large tails.

Serena was looking at their skin. "I wonder what type of predator gave the Lumps those long, straight cuts?"

Most of the dugongs had strange wounds along their backs, now healed.

Ridge looked closely. "I can't think of any creature that makes wounds like that."

"I can." Relm swam up from behind, "Well, it isn't a creature. Do you know what cutters are?"

Serena's eyes grew wide, "Cutters?"

"Yeah, you know, on the back of fast skywhales."

"Oh, we call them spinners." Serena chirped. "Do you think slowspeakers created those injuries with spinners?"

"They seem so slow, how would they be able to get out of they way?"

Relm was talking about the propellers from speed boats. Serena remembered the lesson about spinners from her mother. It was possible the Lumps might have gotten hit by them. Of course, asking the dugongs was impossible. They hardly made any sounds at all, much less speak any form of language.

They were funny though, and Neo had a blast trying to imitate their slow roll-ing-over motions. The dugongs didn't pay much attention to the dolphins. They ate the sea grass beds and floated in slumber.

As the dolphins traveled north, they encountered many different types of dolphins. There were dolphins with spots, and dolphins that spun, achieving acrobatics that even Neo could not accomplish no matter how hard he tried. The spinners only laughed at his feeble attempts to match the five-rotation spin through the air that even the youngest of them accomplished with little effort.

As Serena, Neo, Ridge, and Relm swam along an enormous seaside cliff on the west coast of Australia they came upon the strangest dolphins they had ever seen. Serena greeted the group of five females.

"What are you doing?" squeaked Serena.

She was looking at a dolphin who looked almost like herself in every dol-phin feature aside from a longer beak and a few speckles. These dolphins were also much smaller, almost half the size of Serena and Neo. The strange thing about this dolphin was that she was wearing an enormous sea sponge on the end of her beak. Ridge was incredulous that a dolphin would deliberately hang a dead animal on its snout, but all the dolphins were wearing them. The dol-phin, surprised by the larger newcomers, threw off her sponge and opened her mouth threateningly towards Serena. The other dolphins showed their support by chanting her name.

"Eve, Eve, Eve."

Serena backed off not wanting to start a fight, although Ridge was making some nasty noises from the back.

"We've traveled a long way, friends. We didn't mean to invade your terri-tory. We will only pass through. But tell me, are you only playing with those sponges, or do they serve you some purpose?"

The other dolphins, who in Serena's opinion looked ridiculous wearing sponges, laughed at her.

"Ever hear a dolphin talk like that? Waste air, I think," trilled one of the dol-phins.

"Right, Musgrave. Sponges not toys, sponges protect. Want get stung?"

Serena realized these dolphins had a different dialect. They seemed to speak very simply; most of them were perfectly quiet. They had a body language that was different as well. Eve spoke up as the other dolphins laughed behind her.

"Dolphins' sponge foraging. Don't go too far down without them."

The dolphin group turned away fast and swam off, bubbles streaming in laughter at Serena.

"Well, that was weird," chirped Neo.

Serena chirped her thoughts, "In these clear waters, maybe talking isn't needed as much as in murky waters. Maybe they use body language more."

"Why wouldn't we be able to dive without sponges on our beaks?" Relm questioned. "I mean that is just ridiculous."

"Not really, look down." Ridge replied.

She was already in an upside down, vertical position casting down to the ocean floor. At first there seemed only to be a thick layer of plant life coating the bottom, but beneath it, and under the sand, life was teeming. Serena saw the hiding fish as her casting returned. She took a quick breath and dove straight to the bottom.

"Wait, Serena!" Ridge cried.

Serena smashed her jaws through the weeds into the sand, rooting around for food, when suddenly a searing pain pierced her skin. Her mouth seemed on fire, as if she'd bitten a stone fish. She raced to the surface, her mind blazing with pain. She sucked in a breath, and smacked her beak on the surface of the water. It seemed to help, so she continued smacking her head up and down on the surface. Relm circled underneath uneasily, and whistled continuously for Serena to tell her what happened. Neo was unsuccessfully trying to hold back his laughter at Serena, who looked ridiculous slapping her head around. Ridge, however, was still at the bottom examining the spot where Serena was attacked. There she found something she had never seen before.

In the sea grasses lived a community of tiny stinging organisms that clung to the grasses in huge waves. Casting them only revealed thick grasses. They blended in perfectly as if they were a part of the vegetation. Serena had recovered from her momentary panic and understood why the other dolphins were using sponges.

"They are protecting themselves so they can forage on the ocean floor. What a great idea! Let's go see if we can find some sponges for ourselves."

The others agreed, except for Ridge, who thought that there were other places they could hunt. After a few hours, Neo, Relm, and Serena had found their dead sea sponges, and ripped them up off the sea floor. Serena placed her jaws inside the natural cup opening and dove to the bottom. She surfaced in frustration.

"How do they use these things?" she complained, "If it covers my mouth I can't eat anything, and every time I move quickly, it falls off."

Relm immediately gave up after she was stung trying to push the sponge in front of her through the grass. After several more attempts, Serena found the trick was to only put the sponge on her top jaw and hold it with her teeth. By shaking her head back and forth she moved the sea grass out of the way without getting stung. Then it was as simple as stunning the fish in the sand with a casting blast, and scooping up the meal with her lower jaw. Neo also learned the technique, but Ridge still thought there were other ways to catch a fish.

They continued towards the shore following a group of the long-beaked bottlenose. Serena was reluctant to give up her sponge, so she swam around with it. Neo discovered it was fun to ram Ridge with his sponge and a game of chase began. After being rammed with the sponge several times, Ridge whipped around and grabbed the sponge right off of Neo's snout! They leaped and splashed and finally settled on a game of toss the sponge.

Relm swam ahead as a scout this time. She was now fully healed from her shark attack with the exception of a white scar. She returned after a while to tell Serena her news.

"Serena! I've found a great place to hunt! I followed a group of dolphins into very shallow water with clumps of sea grasses. I cast and discovered that each clump was full of little fish. The long-beaked dolphins seemed to have a strategy to get those fish out of the thick grasses."

"Great!" Serena rubbed Relm's flipper. The dolphins swam in the direction Relm just came from.

"What was the hunting method they used, Relm?"

"The dolphins swam into formation around a clump of grass. One dolphin swam directly over it and fluke splashed with her tail creating a loud, ker-plunk!" Relm swiped her tail at the water's surface.

"Kerplunk?" Neo chuffed.

"Yeah! The fish in the grass scattered, frightened by the noise. They swam right into the mouths of the dolphins."

Serena, it seemed, had taken on the role of matriarch quite easily. Although she missed the thrill of scouting, somehow it wouldn't feel right to leave Neo, Ridge, and Relm alone. They avoided the other dolphins and swam to the shallows. Ridge loved this new game. She volunteered most of time to be the 'ker-plunker'. Relm freaked out as a sea snake darted out of the grass into her open mouth. She chomped down and spit it out. The snake was dead but Neo thought it would make a good toy, so the hunting was put on hold for a while until Neo got bored of chasing Serena around with the maimed sea snake.

Serena loved hunting. She loved discovering new hunting techniques. To her there was nothing better than the thrill of the hunt. The excitement, the anticipation, the power. Hunting was almost better than eating. Which is why she was haunted by what she saw when her party had reached the shores of Monkey Mia.

CHAPTER 7

Monkey Mia

A commotion of splashing and high-pitched squeaks roused the attention of Serena who was swimming just off shore.

"Me, me, me, give it to me!"

Serena heard the calls and thought a game was in progress up near the shore.

"Come on, follow me, let's go investigate the game," she chirped to Neo, Ridge, and Relm.

The four dolphins took off for shore. They were in very shallow water, but the other dolphins were still farther up. Serena cast forward which made her stop in her wake.

"What is it, Serena?" asked Relm.

Serena cast again along with the other three. The echoes resulted in seeing five dolphins in such shallow water that they were basically lying on the sand, but held their heads out of the water.

"Serena," Relm called. "There is something strange in the water."

"It looks like the dolphins are surrounded by thick tree roots," Neo guessed.

Serena echolocated. They were not tree roots. They were part of an animal. Serena received an image of skin with bone inside. She brought her head out of the water to spyhop. Her eyes widened in fear. No more than a few yards away slowspeakers stood on two long legs in the shallow water. The dolphins were sitting in front of them, heads up, whistling, cooing in affection. The slowspeakers were giving the dolphins fish! Dead fish. They were rubbing the dolphins' backs. Baby dolphins zipped around their legs, fearless, grabbing fish when they fell. When a person ran out of fish, the dolphins' loyalty ended, and they moved on to the next fish dangler.

Relm moved forward, keen on getting some of that fish. But a sharp whistle from Serena stopped her.

"Relm, stay here. We cannot be sure it is safe."

"Let's go then, Serena." Neo complained, "I getting hungry looking at all that fish."

"You just ate a full belly's worth this morning!" Serena chirped. "Spread out, look around, but don't get too close to the slowspeakers."

Serena watched all morning.

She and Neo watched the dolphins in the shallows while Ridge and Relm went exploring.

"It seems the slowspeakers only feed those three females and one of the female's calves," Neo ventured.

"Yes, the one with the jagged tipped dorsal fin, and the one with the jagged edge along the back of her dorsal fin. They seem to work as a team, traveling from one slowspeaker to the other."

"Look, other dolphins are sneaking in and getting a few fish, but those three females get the most. I wonder why the slowspeakers only feed those dolphins?"

Serena cruised over towards Ridge and Relm. They were in a deeper area where slowspeakers swam around, looking at the dolphins swimming by. Relm shrieked when she saw one particularly enormous human.

"I didn't know they got that big," she chirped as she swam in the other direction.

In late afternoon the slowspeakers had left the water and the dolphins began to move offshore. Serena caught up with one of the females who had been successfully begging for food. The female turned around and introduced herself with a series of chirps.

"I'm Puck, and this is Piccolo, my calf."

Although Serena was easily ten years younger than this female with a calf, she assaulted her with loud, high pitched shrills, "How could you do that? Accepting dead fish, and from them! How can you call yourself a dolphin? How can you teach your calf to beg? How can you not hunt?"

Serena felt herself rapidly becoming more furious. She had watched all day in amazement, but now the significance of what was occurring had enraged her. This female didn't hunt, she didn't teach her calf to hunt. How could she deny her calf the joy, the freedom of hunting? How could she deny herself the very essence of being a dolphin?

The female was stunned, but replied calmly and lazily, "You not from here, are you. We live here, eating fish over thirty years. Three generations learned secrets of this place. It's still hunting, only using a different way. Fishholders have chosen to feed me and my two friends. They only give fish to us." She said this pointedly as if to discourage Serena from trying.

"My mother showed me here when I was calf. Back then they used to feed everybody. But now only us."

"But aren't the slowspeakers dangerous?" Serena asked.

"Slowspeakers? You mean the fishholders, some call them softrubs. They have soft skin, like us. They like to rub our skin, though it can be overwhelming sometimes. They never hurt us, and calves are safe around them."

Serena could not understand. She saw the slowspeakers kill her entire migration group in a matter of minutes, and here the dolphins were fed by them and let the calves swim freely around them? Serena told the female about the slowspeakers that caught and killed all the dolphins from her migration group, she told her about Tanglers. The female did not know what to make of the story.

"Well, there is nothing like that around here. Life is better and easier with the fishholders around."

Serena was getting frustrated by this dolphin's seeming lack of concern, and her laziness.

She said to the female, "You have forgotten who you are. You have forgotten what it means to be a dolphin. Wild, free, a hunter. You deny your calf the joy of hunting. You deny your calf her freedom!"

At this the older female swung her tail and popped Serena hard in the face.

"You don't know how hard it is to be a mother. You're upset the fishholders refused to feed you. Why waste energy and my calf's on hunting all day when food is so easily gotten? My calf still hunts in the evenings. Being dolphin is surviving and teaching your calves how to survive. I've found my way, now go find your own!"

With that she swam away, calf in tow.

Serena was livid. Her own confusion of what she was doing here hundreds of nights away from home fueled her irritation of these lazy, begging dolphins. Serena may not know her way yet, but she did know that life here at Monkey Mia was not for her.

"I would rather starve then beg for dead fish from a slowspeaker."

With a sharp whistle Serena called her friends to her. "We're leaving this shore, let's go north. These dolphins are no fun, and this place is crawling with slowspeakers."

Neo chirped up, "These slowspeakers don't seem too bad, Serena. They don't want to hurt dolphins, they seem to want to play."

He turned his head towards the shore and watched two young children splashing around making a racket of sounds.

"I thought you wanted to find a place where the slowspeakers would not interfere with dolphin life, Neo?" Serena squeaked, "The slowspeakers dull the minds and hearts of these dolphins. They make them forget that being a dolphin is more than mere survival and getting an easy meal."

Ridge swam up into the conversation, "Then what is being a dolphin about, Serena? Why are we out here? We've spent half a cycle traveling, which is more than any dolphin normally attempts.

"We've eaten food that is strange to us, swam through cold waters, deep waters, and risked death and starvation. Relm may not survive another shark attack, and we haven't found a new group to join in all this time. I miss my home waters. I've found out more about slowspeakers than I ever wanted to know. Let's go home."

"Yes," whistled Relm, "Home."

Serena looked at her friends. Neo, Ridge, and Relm had risked their lives following her, believing that she would find them what they sought. Neo was looking for a place to live where he could be independent and find his place in society. Ridge was looking for a new group to call her own, so she could feel like a member of a family again. Relm was looking for security and love, a comfortable place reminiscent of her nursery. What was Serena looking for? She wanted all the same things that her friends wanted. Home, love, security. She wanted to go home to her nursery. She wanted to protect them. She wanted to protect all dolphins. She wanted to learn about the slowspeaker dangers and tell everyone about them.

The images of the Tangler attack so many months ago now played themselves over in Serena's memory. She remembered the dolphins that knew of the Tanglers and had not passed their knowledge. She thought of the slowspeakers that gave dead fish to the dolphins, and she thought of the little girl who watched her with mutual curiosity.

She turned to the others, "What are these creatures about? Their very nature seems hypocritical and mysterious. They are indiscriminate killers and are at once weak in the water. They scare dolphins away with loud noises, and then bring them in close to feed them fish.

"How can we possibly hope to protect ourselves when we don't know which slowspeakers are friendly and which ones are not?"

Neo, Ridge, and Relm did not have any answers. The complexity of the humans disturbed Serena. Whatever the answer, the search had to continue. So Serena decided to continue north and make their way back towards the Great Rivers that would carry the dolphins home once more.

The dolphins reached the Philippines without incident of man or shark. These South Asian waters were full of life. Serena had never seen so many different species of whales and dolphins. Serena and her group swam along side Dwarf sperm whales, pilot, and melon-headed whales. Spotted, Spinners, Risso's, and Frasier's dolphins all hunted here. It was January and summer time on this side of the world. Serena stayed in shallow waters near the shorelines. Skywhales were everywhere. Most of them were small and low to the water. Neo went up to a few of them curious to know if they would give them anything. Serena stayed back, however, and waited for Neo to bring news.

"They won't give me anything, Serena, but they have large objects that click at me."

"Click at you!? What do they say?"

Serena wondered if the slowspeakers were communicating.

"Nothing, no speech. Just clicks and bright flashes, like the sun coming through water, but only for a second."

Neo was describing a dolphin watching boat and tourists taking pictures of him. This news confused Serena. So far she'd seen slowspeakers that sent loud bangs into the water, killed with Tanglers, played with toys, fed dolphins fish, and now some were clicking and flashing light at them. What was all this about? The reason for starting this journey was the same reason she would continue it. She would compose a great Epic, to teach dolphins about slowspeakers all around the sea.

CHAPTER 8

Drift Net

The dolphins continued north. Land slowly shrank into the distance until it could not be seen at all. Serena, Neo, Ridge, and Relm went hunting with a group of Risso's dolphins. They had never seen dolphins that looked this way. They were large; larger than Serena. The Risso's were robust, blunt headed, and their melons were white with scars. Their dorsal fins were sharply curved back and their flippers were dark gray. Serena led her party as they tailed the Risso's on a hunt.

"Stay back. We don't want to get into a fight. They'll show us the way to food and we'll take what we can."

Ridge opened her mouth menacingly towards the Risso's.

Neo gurgled, "I think its funny you think you can challenge the whitemelons."

"They don't seem so tough to me."

"I'm so hungry, I could eat a whole school," squeaked Relm.

The whitemelons seemed to have honed in on a meal. They were moving into a hunting formation and whistling at each other. Serena leapt out of the water to get a good idea of where they were heading. Land was too far away to see, but a flock of sea birds was circling near the surface.

"I see it!" Serena squeaked. "Now we'll just wait for the whitemelons to round them up and we'll join in. Ridge, Relm, you take the right side. Neo and I will take the left."

The dolphins moved gracefully to either side, flanking the Risso's group. Just within echolocation range of the intended meal the Risso's suddenly stopped their swimming pattern, and slowed to a snail's pace. The buzzing from the group filled the water. Serena also cast forward and was surprised and confused by the resounding echo. Hundreds of fish were dead or in distress up ahead. Serena saw the picture in her mind. The fish were all struggling as if they couldn't swim anymore. Serena looked above the water and saw the birds circling the struggling fish.

"Strange," clicked Relm after casting the fish, "It's as if they hit a cliff wall."

"Only there's no wall," clicked Ridge.

Serena had a bad feeling about this. But she continued to follow the cautious Rissos. Serena's heart began to pound; she didn't trust the safety of the Risso's group.

"Pull together," she trilled to Neo, Ridge, and Relm.

The four dolphins huddled closely as they approached the struggling fish. The answer to the mystery became clear.

"A Tangler!" shrieked Relm.

The four dolphins halted and watched as the Risso's swam right up to the net. Serena screamed out warnings, but they ignored her. The Risso's carefully picked fish out of the tangles of thin plastic rope for an easy meal.

"They are not afraid!" Relm squeaked.

"They've seen this before." Serena guessed. "The whitemelon's know to be careful and not touch the Tangler. Look, the calves are kept away. They are not allowed to eat here."

"Why is a Tangler here?" Ridge asked. "There are no slowspeakers anywhere nearby!"

Neo was taking in the vastness of this net, "Look, Serena. It floats to the surface and then sinks way down."

"How wide is it?" bubbled Serena with wide eyes.

"I don't know, farther than I can cast."

"Let's find out," Serena chirped.

Keeping a distance just close enough to see the netting, the dolphins swam along side of it looking for the end. Strewn up in the net were thousands of fish, sharks, stingrays, eels, octopus, squid, and worst of all to Serena's eyes, dolphins, and even whales. The water was silent in an eerie atmosphere. The net continued on for over a mile. A giant sperm whale floated dead in the water. Its tail was wrapped in the great net. It looked like it had been there for a while. Huge chunks of its flesh were missing where sharks had scavenged. Relm swam away after she came across a female spotted dolphin wrapped in the net, and just behind her was her calf, drowned after following her mother into the web. Serena had never seen so much death in one place.

"It's a Tangler set adrift," Serena bubbled. "A wall of death that is almost invisible until it is too late. Why would the slowspeakers leave this here?"

Serena was having a difficult time thinking about the ways of the slowspeakers. She knew objects could be left behind where they do not belong. All this death was pointless, like the deaths of her migration company. The net was so unnatural, it did not belong. The sea does not have walls, yet here one was, stopping everything in its path. Serena was absently staring at the net when Ridge called for help. One sharp whistle was all it took to send Serena flying in her direction. Neo was approaching the top of the net where a dead whitemelon was floating. He was getting too close.

"Stop him, Serena!" Ridge cried out.

"Neo!" Serena whistled, "Neo, get away from it now!"

But Neo wasn't listening to Serena; he was listening to the faint heartbeat from the Risso's dolphin. Serena swam closer.

"Her heart is beating!" he called out.

A short, raspy breath came from the whitemelon's blowhole, barely noticeable. She was alive. Neo's eyes opened wide. The Tangler was wrapped around the whitemelon's tail. Her skin was sunburned where her body floated out of the water. Her flukes were bleeding where the net was too tight. The Risso's eyes opened a little to look at Neo. They were glossy and showed no emotion.

Neo looked at the net chaining the dolphin, "I have to set her free. Do not worry, whitemelon, I'll get you out."

Neo approached the net.

"Neo!" cried Serena again, but he was ignoring her.

He was right next to the net now, and he began biting it. Ridge swam up to Serena.

"He's going to get his beak stuck in that thing. Stop him!"

Serena edged closer and saw Neo biting at the net, trying to tear it.

"Neo, what are you doing?"

"She is alive!" Neo whistled.

Serena looked at the dying Risso and back at the struggling Neo. He was determined. Ripping with his teeth, Neo tried to slice through. It wasn't easy. The net was tougher than anything he had mouthed before. The drift net was not simply rope. It was made of a tough monofilament, like thick fishing line. Serena knew there was little hope of the helping the whitemelon, even if they could get her free. But Neo was not going to let her die a prisoner and all Serena could do was help or get out of the way. Serena grabbed the net with her teeth. She pulled the rope taught.

"Try again, Neo."

Neo whipped his head viciously back and forth trying to saw through the net. Finally, one piece snapped.

He bubbled in frustration, "There are a hundred more to go. This whitemelon probably spent days biting at the net, only to still be caught."

"Her tail, Neo," Serena chirped. "Bite the ones wrapping her tail."

Serena pulled on the line at the Risso's flukes making the line taught. The Risso weakly trilled in pain as the line cut into her wounds. Neo chomped down on the line with his sharp teeth that fit together like a zipper, and snapped it. Two more, three more. The net was loosening up. Encouraged, Neo took a quick breath. Serena suddenly realized that there was an audience. The group of whitemelons was watching.

Serena was now fully invested in saving the whitemelon too. She wasn't concerned that the Risso might still die of her injuries. She would not die a prisoner of this Tangler. Serena pulled the net trying to loosen it more. Neo tore at it with his teeth. Neo and Serena pulled on the net one final time, and although the net sliced through the edges of the Risso's tail, she was freed.

She floated without moving at first. Serena cast her wounds. The pain in her tail must have been was terrible. The whitemelon slowly moved towards the other waiting Risso's dolphins who called to her. They whistled and trilled and some rubbed her, but they gave her room and together the entire group swam away, west towards the shore. Serena was exhausted but happy. She felt a sense of accomplishment, and she hoped the whitemelon would recover. Serena called out for Relm and Ridge.

"We're here." Ridge called just beyond sight. "I'm with Relm. She doesn't want to look at the Tangler. Should we follow the whitemelons?"

"No," whistled Serena. "Let's just get out of this area. I have a bad feeling about the slowspeakers around here."

The dolphins swam along until they reached the end of the net. Then they headed north. Neo was more alert then usual after leaving the Tangler behind. Serena noticed the change. Neo wasn't as playful as he was before. He was quiet and serious. He was casting ahead all the time.

"Neo," Serena chirped, "Do you see anything up ahead?"

"Not yet, Serena." he replied. "You know, for the first time I feel a responsibility to defend you girls. After helping the whitemelon, I don't know. It feels good to help. I'll never let anything happen to you, Serena."

Serena bubbled. Neo seemed too intense to be serious. But as Serena watched him the next few days it did seem the change was real. Serena hoped that they would never again see a Tangler for the rest of their lives. As she led the group of young dolphins towards the southern coast of Japan, Serena hoped that safety and peace could be found there. She did not realize the perils before her would be the worst yet.

CHAPTER 9

Follow the Rising Sun

Neo and Relm swam together just behind Serena and Ridge. They were traveling north, hoping to find an Eastern current they could ride towards home. Neo was singing to pass the time; no words, just a melodic whistling and chirping that filled the silent void of the open ocean. His song comforted the girls and Serena remembered her mother singing to her many cycles ago. Relm took up her own melody in a sweet high pitched whistle.

Knowing is to believe another
Remembering is to tell all you know
Learning is to watch each other
Growing is to discover on your own.

"I remember a song my mother sang," Ridge trilled. "This was one of my favorites, and I'm glad to sing my mother's Epic song to you."

If you're strong, you will be a leader
Becoming wise through living years.
I will die to save another
I will shine and show no fear.

Neo bubbled at that one, "I think that Epic was noble."

He sang it again in his own melody and all four trilled together, singing melodies for a while. Finally, Serena made up a new part of the song to reflect her own adventure.

Into the Blue, an unknown journey.
We will find our Epic song.
Remember our family, we'll live in harmony.
Through many dangers our friendship grows strong.

The young dolphins played around a while, chasing each other and forgetting they were on the opposite side of the world from their home. They were having such a good time that it was nearly Black before they realized they hadn't found anywhere to hunt yet.

"I'm so hungry," Neo suddenly realized and he cast around for a hint of food.

"I love hunting at night," Ridge squeaked. "It's a great challenge."

Different animals came up from the depths and they were interesting to look at. Some of them even glowed with their own internal lights.

As the night wore on, Serena was ready to wait until morning.

She was just about to suggest they rest awhile when Relm trilled, "Cast ahead, look! Thousands of them! Rising from the deep."

Serena, Ridge, and Neo furiously cast ahead to see in the dark thousands of squid pursuing their own meals. Serena gave direct instructions for the hunt.

"If we race in they will scatter, and it will be more difficult to find them. Neo and Ridge, you flank the sides and circle them in. Use bubbles to trap them. Relm will blow bubbles from below to bring them to the surface. I'll take over Ridge's position after I grab a few. Ridge can relieve Relm, Relm, you relieve Neo, and Neo will take over for me. We'll keep this pattern until we're done."

Everyone bubbled in agreement. Everything went according to plan, at first. Each dolphin got a chance to eat from the trapped ball of squid and they took turns. Having the plan in advance allowed little communication needed while eating. Because of the darkness, Serena did not bother to open her eyes. Her echolocation told her everything she needed to know about her environment; which is why she knew a few seconds ahead of time that she was not the only predator interested in the squid.

The sharks had arrived and were cutting through the middle of the squid ball without regard to the well made dolphin hunting plan. The squid ball began to break up with the hapless invading sharks thrashing about, so Serena made the decision to leave to the squid to them.

"We don't want to get caught in the middle."

The dolphins hung around the area though, catching stray squid as they escaped the sharks' feeding frenzy. By early morning the squid had attracted many sharks and they seemed to want to hang around even though the food was now totally devoured. A roaring in the distance caught Serena's ear. A sky-whale was approaching. Suddenly Serena and the other dolphins felt a sound pulse being directed at them. As if they were being cast by a hundred dolphins at once. It was a weird feeling and the dolphins became slightly disoriented by it.

"Move away!" Serena called to the others, and the dolphins quickly swam away from the approaching skywhale. The ship increased its speed and the dolphins swam faster trying to out run the ship's underwater sonar system. The Japanese fishing vessel had used sonar to locate its targets. The vessel slowed down as it approached the dolphins. The sonar had shown the fishermen the way to their prey. Serena watched in terror as the boat circled them and a Tangler was being dumped into the sea.

"Fast! Away!" Serena cried.

She led the others down to the ocean floor and swam under the Tangler before it got a chance to ensnare them. Serena swam harder then she had ever swam before, scared to death.

Neo cried out, "Wait, Serena, they are not following us, they don't want us this time. Look!"

Serena reluctantly slowed and turned around. She cast back towards the boat that had now fully stopped and was pulling up the Tangler. The net was full of sharks, the same sharks who had ruined their hunt just a few hours earlier.

Relm cried, "Let's go Serena, I don't want to watch. They could come after us next. We should go."

But Serena could not turn away, she had to see. She had to know what the slowspeakers wanted with all those sharks. They weren't pulling them up the same way the others had pulled up the dolphins, or even the shrimp. They were bringing the Tangler to the side of the skywhale instead of up onto it. Serena swam toward the boat casting ahead of her. Her echo images were confusing, they didn't make sense. The sharks were splashing back down into the water from the boat but they weren't swimming, they were sinking straight down into the depths. Her casting became even more confusing. The sharks were not the shape they were supposed to be, the picture was different. Serena needed to see with her eyes. She swam even closer but stayed deep so the slowspeakers wouldn't see her. Serena's dread turned to horror as she saw the sharks, one by one, fall into the black below.

They couldn't swim because they had no fins. The dorsal fin, the side fins, the tail fins, all had been cut off. Blood followed down after the sharks, leaving dark streaks trailing down into the abyss. Serena swam directly under the sky-whale. She heard Relm and Ridge screaming at her from a distance. She had to know; she had to see what was happening up there. What were the slowspeakers doing? She crept up to the side of the vessel. She popped her head above the surface to look with both eyes. The sky was dark but the moon and lights on the boat provided enough light to see by.

Serena could not believe what she was seeing. The slowspeakers hauling up the net grabbed on to the sharks with enormous hooks, cutting into their sides and hauling them up to the side of the boat. While one man held the shark by the hook, two more used huge knives to slice off all the fins, and then the shark was thrown back into the sea, alive. The sharks were helpless to swim and they sank quickly, eventually drowning.

Serena felt pity for the creatures even though they were predators, scavengers, and nuisances to dolphins. They could not cry in pain, or for help, having no voices. They were not social, and no one was coming to their rescue. All the amazing senses and abilities of the sharks could not help them now, as they were so ruthlessly attacked. Serena swam away mortified. She imagined dolphins in the place of the sharks and could not bear the thought of being thrown back into the sea with no fins or flippers. She never knew the humans were using a technique of fishing called finning, taking only the fins from the sharks and using the fins for shark fin soup, which is a delicacy in Japan and around the world.

Serena rejoined Neo, who was waiting close by, and together they met up with Ridge and Relm. She didn't tell them what she had seen at first. She swam without making a sound for hours. The rest of the night the dolphins swam, with no particular direction or goal in mind. Trapped in her own head, Serena wondered what the slowspeakers wanted with shark fins. What was worth the waste and torture?

She did not want to remember it anymore. She did not want to learn anymore about slowspeakers. She wanted to go home and live in peace. As the ocean surface turned hues of pink and orange, Serena lifted her head into the light. The sun was rising in the East. It looked like it was coming out of the ocean itself. The Ocean turned to liquid gold as Serena squinted in the sunlight. It was time to go home. She must go in the direction of the rising sun, back out into the open blue, and take the eastward currents back to her nursery waters. Serena no longer cared about her Epic song or learning about the slowspeakers, she only wanted to go home. How long had she been gone? Almost a full cycle, she suddenly discovered.

"Serena?" Relm ventured, "Are you alright? You've been quiet."

"It's time to head home now," Serena whistled. "We've been gone too long. None of us have our mothers anymore; we are not calves any longer. We are our own school and we will make our home in my nursery waters."

She turned to face Ridge and Relm.

"You will love it there. Plenty of food, beauty all around, endless games."

She turned towards Neo, "There are many groups you could join and then you could hunt with us anytime."

The other dolphins looked at each other.

"And what about the Epic?" Neo quietly asked.

"I don't want to think about what I have seen. I have seen enough. I have had enough of slowspeakers. I don't care about the Epic."

Neo, Ridge and Relm were silent. Serena turned back towards the Sun.

"You've followed me this far. Will you now follow me home?"

Neo swam up to her side.

"I'll follow you anywhere, Serena. You know that. You are my best friend, and I'll follow you. To keep you out of trouble if nothing else."

"And who will keep you out of trouble, Neo?" Ridge cooed. "I will come with you, Serena. You promised you'd never leave us behind."

Relm chirped, "And I will follow you, Serena, because I want to go home again too."

The four dolphins began their journey home side by side, breathing in synchrony, and singing softly as they entered to open ocean.

The vast desert of the open ocean seemed endless. The dolphins swam with the northern Pacific currents that traveled east. They moved across the Pacific from Japan out into the ocean. Food was scarce and even slowspeaker ships were rare. The dolphins saved their energy and hunted at every opportunity.

"It's too bad there are no Pushers this time," Relm trilled.

She swam just below the surface where the currents were strong.

"A nice big one could save us hours of swimming."

"I am glad we have seen any skywhales," Serena whistled.

The wind had picked up, and the surface was getting choppy.

"After all," Relm continued, "Not all skywhales are dangerous."

"But that's the problem, Relm." Serena whistled, "We cannot tell if they are dangerous or not until it's too late. Best to just stay clear of them."

These waters were colder than the southern waters traveling from the Tuamoto Islands. The dolphins fed mainly at night; that is when animals rose from the depths following the plankton upwards. During the day the blue infinity loomed ahead. Because there was so little to see, anything that turned up became a curiosity.

"A flyer feather!"

Neo grabbed it in his cone shaped teeth. He dragged it along in his mouth, by his flipper, on his dorsal fin, and he even kicked it around with his tail flukes. Ridge and Neo took turns holding the feather and they kept it for two whole days. The dolphins weren't eating nearly enough, but if they just made it a few more days, maybe shallow waters would return. The first hint that land was near was, as always, the sea birds, next, more fish, and third, the skywhales. They had traveled nearly two thousand miles across the Pacific. Serena was so happy to see the ocean floor she dove down and rubbed her entire body in the sand, rolling over and over.

"That crossing wasn't nearly as long as the other ones," chirped Relm. "It only took us fifteen or sixteen Lights and Blacks."

"I wasn't counting," replied Ridge. "They all blur together for me."

The dolphins were off the coast of the big Island of Hawaii.

"Serena," called Neo. "Here come some dolphins."

A group of bottlenose dolphins approached and Serena swam up to greet them. She did not want any trouble.

"Hello, I'm Serena," she whistled. "Up for a hunt?"

She figured if she involved the other dolphins in a hunt they might share some information with her.

"I'm Le'ale'a," squeaked a large female.

Serena was surprised by this dialect of whistles. She understood most of what they said, however.

"Hunting together will be fun! Lele and Pa'a'ni are good scouts. They jump higher and play harder than all others. They'll be back with us soon."

She turned to her school and called them together, "Nai'a! Dolphins! This is Serena, friend, Hoaloha!"

All the dolphins squeaked, "Hoaloha!"

Two dolphin scouts suddenly appeared and the entire school took off with them.

"Let's go!" Serena called to Neo, Relm, and Ridge.

They assisted the school in an exhilarating hunt. The typical block and drive moves were coordinated to round up a large school of silvery fish. After the meal the other dolphins wasted no time in congratulating themselves and each other. The scouts, Lele and Pa'a'ni, were getting most of the fin rubs and Serena remembered her life as a scout, not a matriarch. She had grown so much in the past year.

The water was warm and clear and as Serena was to find out, had the best waves in the world. The dolphins headed for shore and Serena's party followed. As the dolphins approached land the water began to swell up so high it hit a breaking point and curved over creating a crashing white run of water at the surface. One by one the Hawaii dolphins disappeared into the breaking waves.

"Come on!" a young dolphin splashed noisily towards Neo, "I'm Paki'. Ride the waves with us, the higher the wave the faster you go!"

And with that she took off upwards as a swell rose and thrust her forward. Serena watched from underwater as Paki' flattened out her pectoral flippers and tail flukes for a ride through the waves. Neo was so excited he could hardly contain himself.

He swam over to Serena, "Come on. I feel a big wave coming up, let's go!"

Together Serena and Neo beat their tails and headed for the top of the crest. Serena flattened out and let the wave push her forward. It was like bow riding only it was like falling too, and she had to know when to turn around before ending up on the beach. Serena swam back out to catch another one. Relm was the only dolphin hanging back.

"Relm, let's go, ready?" Serena trilled.

"You go ahead, I'll wait here."

"Come on, Relm. If you don't catch a wave, you'll never ride it. And its great fun, I promise. Trust me."

"I trust you, Serena. Will you go with me?"

"Of course! Alright, get ready, here it comes!"

Relm took a deep breath and beat her tail forward until she hit the crest of the wave. She angled her head down and flattened her flippers. Serena and Relm felt the push of the water as they fell forward through the waves. Relm heard Serena whistling near to her.

"Whoo!!"

The water rushed by her face, she opened her mouth and let the water press on her tongue. She laughed, bubbles streaming from her blowhole.

"Alright, Relm, now turn around quick and swim to the bottom!"

Relm followed Serena's instructions and curved out of the wave before getting too shallow. They swam to the bottom and under the wave pressure back out to catch another one. The dolphins continued surfing the Hawaiian waves all day long, even as the sun set behind them.

CHAPTER 10

Songs of the Whales

Spring was a time of movement around the Hawaiian waters. Sea turtles and humpback whales were coming and going. Pilot-whales and spinner dolphins swam together, although the spinners would often leave to ride the bows of skywhales or show off for each other by spinning acrobatically through the air. Serena, Neo, Relm, and Ridge had regained their strength hunting in the plentiful, bright, clear water. There were slowspeakers everywhere here, though they did not seem to care too much about the dolphins. Serena noticed the change in them as a skywhale approached and blew past; the slowspeakers didn't even take a second glance at them.

"Maybe these slowspeakers are different. Perhaps they don't even notice us here." Relm bubbled.

"Let's hope they leave us alone from now on," Serena chirped.

She had seen so many conflicting behaviors of the slowspeakers she didn't know what to think about them anymore. In Serena's opinion the less contact she had the better. The dolphins played in the Hawaiian waters for almost a week. Relm and Ridge seemed content, but Serena wanted to keep moving on. Even Neo seemed impatient to leave. He talked about his nursery waters and was excited about returning home.

He tried to describe it to Relm, "It's like a pocket of sea between two shores, and inside is a paradise. The kelp forests stretch from the sea floor up to the surface creating a canopy of shimmering light. There are so many places to hide and play. There are so many good fish to eat. The other animals there are bigger than anywhere I've seen. Huge rays twice as long as a dolphin, whales that are so big even their calves push water like a skywhale. The water is cool and clear, the perfect nursery grounds. We call it BrightWater."

Neo was talking about the Gulf of California, the same waters Serena had grown up in. That was Neo's home range too. Serena sang an Epic that Neo also knew.

The Western tides bore us,
There is a whisper in the waves.
The water rushes so strong,
The waves call my name,

The Moon shines down from a starry sky.
The Sun shines down in shimmering light.
This paradise is where I belong.
BrightWater will always be my home.

The four dolphins continued chatting as they swam through the clear waters along the East coast of the big island of Hawaii.

"Hey, listen," Serena chirped. "What's that?"

They stopped chirping for a moment and listened to the waters. A low note emerged out of the blue in a grumbling sort of way, then the pitch rose up to a beautiful muted tone.

"What is that?" chirped Relm.

For a while the dolphins just listened as the songs became clear. Each note was arranged into a phrase, each flowing phrase was repeated several times before another was created. Each sequence of phases became a theme. One song contained several themes and the whales repeated their songs over and over again.

After a while Relm became concerned, "It sounds like it's getting closer."

Two dark shadows emerged from the blue. The huge shapes of humpback whales came into view.

"I think we should probably get out of here," Serena began, but suddenly the two enormous whales were upon them, moving faster then Serena would have ever thought possible for such a big creature.

It was two male humpbacks battling for dominance in an impressive display of singing, swimming, and, as Serena was about to find out, fighting. Whoosh! A massive tail plunged down through the water with such immense force that Serena and Neo were blown back.

"Relm, come on, let's go," squeaked Ridge.

The two dolphins tried to swim out of the way, but the humpbacks were oblivious to anyone swimming nearby, and they barreled towards the little dolphins without even noticing them. The bigger male humpback slammed his bulk into the other whale, showing his dominating strength. But the other male was not going to give up so easily. The winner of this fight would get the honor of escorting a female and her calf to the feeding grounds, and hopefully become the father of her next calf. Becoming a father was the most important thing a male humpback could be, so this fight was not a trivial matter. The two whales tilted their heads towards the surface, and Serena and Neo screamed at the top of their lungs to Relm and Ridge.

"Get out of the way!! Move!"

The whales blasted toward the surface and exploded out of the water in a great display of gravity and defiance. The whales' tails were the only part visible from below the water. Ridge looked up just in time to see the two huge bodies crash back down above them. Relm and Ridge split apart swimming in opposite directions just as the two colossal whales tumbled by in a tangle of flukes, blubber, and bubbles. All the while, the intense singing continued.

The four dolphins got back together and swam away as fast as possible from the competing males. Not far away the females and calves were basking in the sun, lazily floating about, and acting as if the rogue males were not stirring up the oceans close by. The whales were large and thickset. On their backs they had a fleshy hump and a small dorsal fin. Serena was most impressed by their very long pectoral flippers, which were one third the length of the whales' bodies. Serena imagined steering and balancing herself with the grace and majesty of these ocean giants.

One of the young humpbacks, only three times the size of Serena, swam nearby looking at them curiously. Up close Serena saw that the big chin of the humpback was rippled, and could expand like a balloon when filled with water. The blowhole of these whales had two spouts instead of just one, like the dolphins have. Serena blew some bubbles at the baby and swirled around to get its attention. The young calf must have decided it was bored and hungry, because it left the staring dolphins and swam underneath its mother to nurse.

The water was soon filled with sound again.

"Oh no," Relm gurgled. "Here they come again!"

Serena looked around at the other whales. They were not moving off or panicking, so Serena felt that they were not in danger.

"Look," Serena chirped, turning towards the sounds. "They are not fighting any more."

The whale song was not the same as the competing whales. This was the whale song of the courting males. Those victorious in battle who had returned to claim their prizes, the right the escort the females and defend them on the long journey across the ocean.

Serena and the others watched as males sung to the females and performed fantastic spins and dives for their amusement. The songs were filled with promises to keep the females and calves safe, and proclamations that they were the biggest, strongest, and the most loyal whales in all the wide oceans. Each female picked a male and allowed him to swim alongside her.

Serena watched with amusement at this silly ritual. What a production the males had to go through, just to attract a mate.

Serena then wondered, 'How would she know how to choose the best mate to ensure a healthy calf?' She knew calves were born in nursery schools with females and calves only, no males. She knew the males joined the groups during big hunts, migrations, and several times during the year when the water temperatures change. Did the male dolphins fight with each other the way the humpbacks did? Serena did not know the answers to those questions. She would need her mother for that, or at least her matriarch, Alatina.

As the dolphins swam around the big humpbacks, Serena thought about Neo. He should be part of a bachelor clan of male dolphins, doing male dolphin things. Should she ask him if he knew about courting?

"Hey, Serena," Neo suddenly chirped, "Let's swim over that big whale's blowhole, and wait until it breathes out, and get rolled around in the bubbles!"

Neo jetted off just as the humpback breathed out. He was enveloped in bubbles and let the rising air push him to the surface.

'No,' Serena thought. 'He would not know anything about courting, he still thinks he's in a nursery.'

Serena sighed, letting air slowly escape from her blowhole, then zipped off to join Neo in the new game they called Bubble Blows.

A few fun days passed by and with seemingly no warning whatsoever, all the newly paired, and unpaired, humpback whales began to move. In a migration formation the whales took off together in a purposeful way that gave Serena an idea.

"Where are they all going?" Relm asked.

"It look's like they are heading directly out to sea." Neo trilled, "It looks like they are headed directly towards…"

"Home."

Serena had a purposeful look in her eye.

"What are you thinking, Serena?" Neo asked.

"I think Serena is about to tell us to say goodbye the warm water islands," Relm cried.

"And say hello to barren, bottomless, open blue." Ridge chirped.

"Where there isn't a fish for days,"

"And the nights are so black even casting shows you nothing,"

"And your stomach hurts so bad you'd eat seaweed!"

"Listen!" Serena cried, "It won't be that way this time! This time we've got a ride, if we hurry to catch it!"

"What are you squeaking about?" Ridge countered, "Skywhales are too fast to ride all the way across."

"Not skywhales! Real whales! We'll ride the whales home!"

At first Serena wasn't sure how the other dolphins felt about the idea. They just stared at her in silence.

Then suddenly Neo burst out, "Yeah! What a great idea! The whales will take us straight across, and we will barely have to swim at all!"

"Of course," Ridge concurred, "Think of the protection we'll have riding with the whales!"

Relm piped in, "Will they care if we ride alongside them?"

"There's only one way to find out. Let's go!"

Serena, Neo, Ridge, and Relm set off to catch up with the whales believing that no dolphin had ever done anything as crazy as ride whales across the sea, when in fact dolphins practiced this quite often. When they reached the whales, the goliaths did not even feign acknowledgement. The humpbacks continued swimming as if on a mission, and the dolphins easily adjusted to the slipstream of the moving whales.

It took them one month to cross the twenty five hundred miles across the Pacific from Hawaii to California. The whales traveled slowly, but they did not stop day or night. The dolphins would often swim ahead to look for food. The pace was slow, but relaxing, and the dolphins were able to rest most of the day. The whales did not seem to notice them, except for a few of the calves who were very curious. When they reached shallow waters, the dolphins chirped farewell to the seemingly oblivious whales.

Serena whistled, "The first thing we do is eat. Let's find a meal fast."

The others were tired, but hungry too, so they all began scouting about for food. They were swimming through forests of kelp. The light of the sun shimmered through the kelp leaves created moving shadows as the dolphins swam in search of a meal. Fish were everywhere, but they were well sheltered in their kelp homes, and it was difficult to catch large numbers. They cast the sandy bottom and each caught several pounds of fish, but they needed much more. Serena decided to move farther into shore in hopes of corralling some school-ing fish.

"Here we go, Neo!" Serena called, "A nice school of silvers, round them up with me?"

"With pleasure!"

The four dolphins easily herded the fish and gobbled them up. A little more full, the dolphins searched around a bit. They swam back toward the kelp for-ests and Neo spotted something odd on the sea floor.

"Hey, girls, look at this!"

Serena approached closer and a strange shape emerged through the green water. An odd irregular shape came into focus, with sharp pieces emerging as if the object had been beaten on rocks and broken. It was once a square but now was crooked and bent. Crustaceans had made homes of this seemingly bit of slowspeaker trash. They were actually old crates and were filled with rocks that weighed them down.

"What on earth is this for?" Serena wondered out loud.

"Look, Serena, there's more." Ridge called. Serena turned and saw that tied to the crates were lines of rope covered in algae that looked like seaweed at first glance. Serena followed the rope to the surface.

Neo unexpectedly cried, "Serena, look out!"

Serena screamed in terror as she swam directly into a fisherman's net! Panic filled her heart and she feared that she was trapped but the net was not around her, only above her. She backed away and thanked Neo. She warned the others to be careful. Relm would not come near but Ridge swam around behind the net and discovered another box.

"This one is shiny, no creatures living on it. It must be new."

Serena swam away a little and turned around to get the full view of the con-traption. Two ropes anchored by the weights held a circular net that headed into the current. The net was long and turned into a tube of netting leading into a cage held up by floating buoys. Ridge peered into the cage and saw some of the kelp forest fish trapped inside. They weren't fish the dolphins would find tasty. Some were brightly colored orange, or had stripes that glinted in the sun-light. Serena tested the cage with her lower jaw and found the metal cold and hard. She opened her mouth and tried to bite it but she couldn't get the right angle. Serena gazed into the cage and saw the little fish struggling to remain stable.

A desire crept into Serena's mind to destroy this trap, not really from a want to save the fish, but more a need to destroy the slowspeakers' snare. She didn't want this net floating here no matter how small it was. Serena bit at the cage again, she pushed it at with her rostrum and it swayed gently in the water. She pushed harder and rammed the tough cage with her head. It rattled around a bit but the net held fast on the cage.

"Come on, Neo, help me get rid of this thing." She squeaked.

Neo started biting at the tough net but it cut up the soft skin on his lower jaw and tongue.

"No use, Serena, the trap is too tough. Let's leave it and get out of here."

Ridge and Relm clicked in agreement. Serena didn't want to give up so easily, she turned tail and fluked the cage hard. She made a dent in it and that seemed to encourage her. Relm chirped out her warning call.

"What's wrong, Relm? I'm only having a little fun."

Serena continued to pummel the makeshift fish trap and ignored the warning cries even as Ridge joined in.

Finally, Neo swam right up into Serena's face and barked, "Serena, listen to us! A skywhale is on the way here. In fact, it's already here. We have to go now!!"

Neo shoved Serena hard in the ribs with his beak to push her away. The skywhale roared above them and came to a stop right next to the trap. The water became oily with the gas from the boat and Relm screamed as she swam off in terror. Serena could not have known that this was an illegal fish trap, meant to catch beautiful, colorful fish to be sold at pet stores.

"Alright, let's get out of here," Serena chirped.

She was too late. A noise filled the water that was so loud Serena became deafened for a moment. The sound was a crack in the water so powerful that Neo was stunned, unable to move.

A second crack through the water came immediately after the first, filling Serena's mind with numbness. She looked up through the water and saw the slowspeakers above her waving their arms frantically. One of them was holding something large and black. Serena recognized it as the same thing that the slowspeaker had the day the migrating dolphin party had stolen the shrimp. It was a blaster, and the human was using it to scare the dolphins away.

One more loud blast filled the water and Serena felt pain like she had never known. At first she thought the pain was caused by the sharp sound in her ears that violently vibrated through her lower jaw and melon. But then Serena saw blood in the water. Her blood. The pain was in her back, just behind her dorsal fin. A searing pain shot through her body like a lightning bolt, as if she had been stung by a thousand stingrays.

Serena screamed and flew through the water not knowing which direction she was going. Her only clear thought in a jumble of pain and panic was to get as far from the skywhale as possible. Only when Neo caught up with her, begging her to slow down, telling her she was safe, telling her the skywhale had not followed, did Serena remember her friends. She slowed and felt the pain again, like fire in her tail. She came up and took a quick breath. Relm and Ridge swam up beside her. She felt herself being cast as her friends checked her for injuries. Ridge came closer and echolocated Serena where she had a great wound.

"Well," Serena trilled, "how bad is it?"

Neo swam before her to look into her eyes.

"It is a small hole in the base of your tail. It's bleeding pretty badly. I don't know how you got it though. I couldn't see anything, that loud bang nearly blinded me. You'll be alright though, Serena."

Neo rubbed his rostrum softly along Serena's chin. Ridge was chirping rapidly to Relm who chuffed in shock.

"What is it, Ridge. What's wrong?" Serena whistled.

"Serena, you have something inside you. I don't know what it is. It's like a small stone, smooth on the edges and sharp at one point. It's stuck inside you, it can't come out."

Serena had been shot and the bullet was lodged in muscle in her left side, just behind the dorsal fin. Neo rushed over to the wound and echolocated for himself. He pushed his beak against the wound, thinking he could push it out, but Serena jolted in pain. She was losing too much blood. Serena thought fast. She knew she would be attracting sharks.

"Come on. Let's swim toward shore. I'll be alright, but I want to leave before the sharks get here."

Serena led the others through the water. Neo stayed right by her side. Relm and Ridge continued to cast Serena's body and the surrounding waters. After a long while the dolphins had made it to shore. They were in shallow waters once more. Serena had continued to bleed steadily and though she didn't tell the others, she was feeling very weak, so weak she could hardly move. But she kicked her flukes hard, fighting against the pain, and rested one eye while using the other one.

"Serena, below us!!" Relm cried out.

Serena looked down and saw the dark shape of a shark below. They had tracked her, and now they had found her. How had it come to this? So close to home, only to be so careless and stubborn. Killed by the slowspeakers, after she had escaped them so many times.

'No,' thought Serena, 'not yet.'

She looked down at the growing number of sharks shadowing her below. She closed her eyes and a strange sensation seemed to awaken within her. It was telling her not to open her eyes. To keep them closed and never open them. To rest now, sleep completely in peace. Give in. Sleep. Die.

"No!!" Serena cried out loud as she opened both of her eyes. "I won't let them have me. I won't be shark food."

Serena turned and headed for shore.

"Serena!! Where are you going?"

Neo raced to catch up.

"I can't make it, Neo, I've lost too much blood. The sharks will follow us until I die, they might even come after you. I'm going where they can't get me, where I can rest."

"No, Serena!! We'll fight them off. Don't give up now. I need you, Serena. Please, I have no home without you. You are my home, Serena. Wherever you are is my home. Please don't do this!"

"I'm so tired, Neo, so tired," Serena calmly chirped. "I can't keep my eyes open very much longer. I barely have the energy to breathe."

She surfaced and took in a raspy breath.

"No, Serena. I won't let you do this. You will not beach yourself."

Serena had reached the beach. Waves broke over her limp body. Ridge and Relm powered themselves through the surf to Serena and Neo.

"Come back!" called Relm.

Ridge trilled, "Any farther and we'll get stuck on the beach! Come back! Serena!!"

Serena's belly hit sand. A wave crashed over her and pushed her farther up the beach. Ridge and Relm followed her as far as they could, but panicked when their bellies hit the sand. They pushed hard and swam back out towards the deeper water. Neo stayed.

"Neo, go back." Serena rasped. "You can make it home, to BrightWater. You can live and form an alliance and be strong, the strongest dolphin who swam across the ocean and back again."

"No, Serena. I am only strong because of you. And if you are going to stay up here and dry out, so am I. I won't leave you, Serena. I love you."

"Go back!" screamed Serena.

"No!" screamed Neo.

Both the dolphins had now washed up so shallow that the water flowed back with every wave, leaving them completely on the beach. What they did not realize was that they had washed up on a popular recreational beach for humans. Neo screamed and his eyes grew wide as he saw a dozen slowspeakers running up to him. The slowspeakers surrounded the dolphins and Serena felt cold hands all over her.

'So,' she thought, 'this is what happened to my mother.'

It was true; the slowspeakers had attacked her on the beach, just as Anu had said. That seemed like another life, life with the nursery school so long ago. Serena was still. She had no energy to fight the humans off. She rolled her eye around to Neo who was also surrounded by slowspeakers. One of them seemed to be the leader. It was pointing and slowly directing the others. Neo was being pushed back out to the water! The slowspeakers were pushing Neo back into the waves.

Neo was putting up a huge fight. Serena saw that Neo was struggling to make a tough decision. He should be trying to get away from the people and swim out to Ridge and Relm, but he was fighting to stay with her.

Serena wondered, 'Why were they pushing him back out into the surf? Why were they not pushing her out into the water too? Could they understand that she was hurt and he wasn't?

Neo struggled against the slowspeakers smacking one in the legs with his tail and butting another with his bony beak. He jaw popped at their knees. Serena heard Ridge and Relm calling him from just beyond the waves. She knew he could be free, all he had to do was leave her.

"Go, Neo."

"Serena! Serena!" Neo called.

But she did not answer. Relm and Ridge were calling him back. Twenty human hands were pushing him out to sea. Serena saw Neo through the many long human legs. He had stopped struggling. Serena turned her head away and lay motionless on the beach.

Neo whistled out to her, "Serena, I'll miss you."

Neo swam out into the waves amid the cheers of the slowspeakers.

Serena tried to cry out, "I love you too!" But she was so weak, only a gurgle came out of her blowhole. Slowspeakers were all around her pouring water onto her back. Serena closed her eyes. She wanted to sleep, she was so tired. She was jolted awake by a flash of pain in her back as the slowspeakers put their hands on her wound. A huge vehicle rolled up on the beach in front of Serena. She could not see very well but she saw more slowspeakers coming towards her. She felt cold hands all over her now, she was sure they would kill her soon. Then she felt pressure all around her body. She was being lifted! Lifted out of the sand! They lowered her onto a mat that felt soft on her belly. Then she was being lifted again, and she was squished inside a cloth wrap.

Being lifted out of the water hurt her ribs. Serena felt gravities' pull for the first time. Her stomach hurt. She tried to take a breath but her weight was pushing on her lungs making it very hard to take in air. She was being lifted onto the vehicle. Someone was holding her tail, but she did not have the strength to struggle. She felt better as she was lowered onto a soft foam mat on the back of the truck.

A slowspeaker was right by her head and Serena got a really close look at one. This slowspeaker had light skin and hair. The slowspeaker lowered its head toward Serena and looked her in the eyes. It made some noise but Serena scarcely heard it. Serena closed her eyes and tried to imagine herself somewhere else, home, in the wide open blue. No cares in the world but finding the next hunt, the next adventure. Never doubting your place in the world, never fearing that your friends would leave. Always feeling welcome, important, and a part of this world. Serena remembered a lesson from her matriarch,

> Our friendship is an energy that flows through each of us. Energy can never be destroyed. It can only change forms. Your energy will pass through all that lives in the Oceans.

Remembering these words Serena was not afraid anymore. She was in the unknown surrounded by predators. But Serena thought of her friends and knew they were safe. That was all that mattered to her. She took another raspy breath. She felt cool water being misted onto her drying skin. It felt good. She opened her mouth and they sprayed the cool water onto her tongue. Serena felt the vibrations of the moving truck, and felt the strange new sensation on her skin as the slowspeakers gently rubbed and patted her.

After what seemed like a midlight the slowspeakers lifted Serena up again, squishing her in the stretcher, and carrying her off the truck. After a bit of jostling she felt she was being tipped on her side. Serena was falling and then she was submerged back in saltwater. It was like being born again. She felt the cool water all around her. All the pressure on her lungs and stomach immediately lifted. She almost forgot she was hurt. She pumped her tail to swim out to sea, but felt sudden pain. This time in two places; one, in her tail where she had the bullet wound, and two, in the front of her face, where she hit the wall of the pool she had been dropped into.

CHAPTER 11

Walls and Reunions

Serena swam rapidly around the edges of the pool, circling and circling, there was no way out. She quickly became exhausted and floated to the surface. Her eyes closed again and her thoughts became fuzzy. She wondered what was going to happen to her and she hoped it wouldn't be too painful. She wanted to sleep again, only it seemed the slowspeakers would not give her time. She was awakened by a rumbling sound and a high pitched squeaking noise coming from below her. The floor of the pool was rising, slowly and steadily. Serena did not have the energy to fight it. She took another painful, raspy breath. She was lifted completely out of the water now and slowspeakers surrounded her once again. They sat beside her with their hands on her back and held onto her tail tightly. Gravity pulled on her once again and she felt heavy. She never realized how large slowspeakers were. One towered over her, she only saw up to his knees. He knelt down in front of her and placed on the ground a group of shiny, sharp objects.

Serena's eye was immediately attracted to the long shiny thing that looked like a long tooth. A sense of dread filled her heart, and Serena feared what this thing would be used for. But before she could truly panic her mouth had been forced open and a rubber tube was pushed down her throat. Serena felt the strangest sensation of the tube going down into her body and her stomach filling with some liquid food. She took a raspy breath through her blowhole and closed her eyes. She did not have the energy to fight. After a minute or so the tube was removed and her mouth released. Then she looked to her side and the shiny, sharp object was gone.

Just as Serena wondered where it had gone, she felt a sharp pain on her tail where the wound was. She squeaked out in pain as the humans gave her a shot. Soon the pain began to go away. She felt calm and soothed. Her tail didn't hurt anymore. In fact, she couldn't feel her tail at all. Serena had been given food with a mild tranquilizer to calm her and her tail had been injected with an anesthetic to numb her tail. She didn't feel any pain as the veterinarian surgically removed the bullet lodged in her side. She didn't realize that the humans had taken a blood sample from her. She didn't know that she had been given antibiotics and vitamins to help her heal.

The slowspeakers finally left her alone. The pool bottom lowered and submerged her back in the water. She swam around for a while in a daze until the tranquilizer wore off. Her tail began to ache again, but she found that she had more energy now. She swam in circles, and was careful not to touch the walls. Serena needed to rest, so she closed her eyes for a while and tried to stay still at the surface.

When she fully awoke her mind was clear. She took a good look around. The water was unnaturally still, and it was very quiet. She heard a small noise and found a hole in the wall blowing out cool water. She noticed a dark leaf standing out on the white bottom of the pool. The walls were blue. She imagined that she was out in the wide open with nothing but blue as far as she could see, but then, as she echolocated in front of her, a large black shape loomed in her mind, and she knew the walls were there.

Later that day, a slowspeaker appeared at the edge of the pool looking down at her. It had a silver pail in its arms. Serena looked up at the slowspeaker and swam a little closer to get a look. Serena heard the slowspeaker make a high pitched whistle and a fish dropped into the water in front of Serena's eyes. Serena was surprised and backed away from it. She cast it and mouthed it. It seemed fresh, it was cold and springy. But it was dead. She spit the fish out and let it sink to the bottom.

She was reminded of the dolphins at Monkey Mia that begged for the dead fish in the shallows. She remembered feeling angry because they were not hunting, they were not doing what dolphins were supposed to be doing. Everything was wrong, and Serena suddenly felt fully her situation. She was not in the ocean, she was being given dead fish, and she was surrounded by land. She had been marooned, captured. And she would not eat the slowspeaker fish. No matter what.

Another fish was dropped into the water. Serena didn't budge. She didn't even turn to look at it. Then she heard the rumbling sounds of the pool floor rising again. She swam around and around, but floor kept rising and she was again stranded out of the water. The slowspeakers surrounded her once more and pushed the rubber tube down her throat. She felt her stomach filling again as the ground up fish mixed with medicine was poured down her mouth. She felt another shot in her side. Then the slowspeakers all left and the she was lowered into the water. No one tried to give her any more fish and she was left alone in the silent pool as the sun disappeared and darkness filled the water.

The first night was the worst in this new home. Serena felt the stillness close in around her, and in the silence her own mind seemed so loud that she whispered to herself in her thoughts. She thought she heard distant dolphin voices sometimes, but then everything would become silent once again. Serena was left alone most of the time but she had to endure forced feedings twice a day for a week. They always tried to feed her and she always refused to eat the dead fish. On her seventh night just as the sun was going down she thought she heard a voice.

"Eat the fish!"

"What?" Serena whistled out, "Is someone there?"

"Eat the fish and you can get out of there."

"Where are you?" she squeaked back.

"Just eat the fish and you can join us!"

"Who are you?!"

After that there came no reply. Had she imagined it? No, it was real. She had heard another dolphin. Was she near the ocean? Serena pondered all night long what the voice meant. How could she escape by eating the fish? She didn't dare try to jump out. Serena had looked over the wall many times and there was nothing but hard, flat rock as far as she could see. Her tail was feeling much better now. If she returned to the sea, surely she would be able to swim strongly.

The next morning, same time as always, the slowspeaker approached the edge of the pool with the silver pail. It tossed a fish into the water. Serena hesitated. Should I take it? What would happen? She heard the motor of the pool bottom begin to run. The floor began to rise. Serena swam forward and took the fish in her mouth. She heard a high pitched whistle, and the floor stopped moving. Serena swallowed the fish. It wasn't bad. It was fresh at least. Another fish landed in front of her. She ate it. Several more fish landed in the pool. Serena swallowed them up. It felt good to have solid food in her stomach. Every time she ate a fish Serena heard a high-pitched whistle.

Then the fish stopped coming. Serena popped her head above the water to see if the slowspeakers were leaving. She saw the slowspeaker at the edge of the pool with the silver pail. Serena looked at her and heard the whistle again. Several fish came flying through the air and landed in front of her. Serena ducked her head to eat them. She waited for more. Nothing came. Serena popped her head up again, heard the whistle and more fish came flying over.

'So it's a game.' Serena decided, 'If I look up, I get fish. Well let's see what they make of this.'

Serena swam quickly around the pool. She jumped up right next to the slowspeaker and landed with a huge crash back into the water sending water over the wall soaking the slowspeaker who disappeared quickly out of sight. Serena laughed until she was too tired to laugh anymore.

Later that night Serena ate more solid fish and they did not raise the pool. The next few days Serena became so bored that she took to searching the pool for leaves. The most exciting time of the day was feeding time. She learned that if she came closer to the edge of the pool she would get groups of fish instead of one at a time. She learned to listen for the whistle because it meant food was on the way. Serena learned to recognize the slowspeakers who fed her. This way she could ignore the ones who didn't have food, and rush over to ones that did.

On the sixth day after Serena started eating fish the floor of the pool began to rise again. Serena didn't understand. She was eating the fish, why was the floor raising again? Serena instinctively gave out a warning cry and struggled as the slowspeakers surrounded her in the water. She was surrounded by the stretcher again and lifted out of the pool. Serena's pectoral flipper was stuck uncomfortably under her body. She closed her eyes and hoped she would be back in the water soon. She felt only a few minutes of discomfort however, because she was soon re-submerged into water.

Immediately a storm of sound hit her ears. Dolphins were conversing all around her, buzzing her with echolocation waves. The sounds seemed to be coming from all around her as they bounced off the walls of the pool. She swam free of the stretcher and braced for impact as she thought the dolphins would be attacking her at any moment. But to Serena's surprise the dolphin's were now all sitting up around the wall of the pool getting fed. A fish fell into the water by Serena's face. Serena snapped it up and looked out of the water. A familiar slowspeaker was standing there with the silver pail. Serena heard the whistle and another fish came flying. Serena caught it in her mouth. She swam closer to the edge like the other dolphins and received more fish. Suddenly all the slowspeakers left and Serena turned to face the dolphins that were in the pool with her. There were only three others, all female. Serena realized she was the not youngest of them. The eldest approached her first as the other two hung back.

"So, what your name young one? I am Alona."

"Serena," she replied.

The female behind Alona abruptly pushed forward, casting Serena. Serena looked closer and realized there was something familiar about this dolphin. She moved a certain way that was familiar.

"Siren," said the female.

That name was familiar to Serena. The voice was familiar. It was a voice that she remembered being very close, a voice that had been quiet, reassuring, loving. For a moment Serena could not grasp the impossibility of her wildest hopes. Then she realized something that had been taken away from her was now returned.

"Mother?"

"Serena!" called the female.

"Mother!"

Once Serena had heard Siren call her name she knew immediately that her mother was swimming before her, alive and safe. They swam towards each other and rubbed sides. Serena felt like a calf again, safe in her mother's slipstream, feeling like no harm could ever come to her.

Siren quickly explained how she was carried off the beach just like Serena.

"I was very sick and should have died, but the slowspeakers kept me alive by feeding me and after uncountable darks and lights alone I became well again. Then other dolphins joined me and together we grew strong again. And now that you are here, Serena, I shall be very happy.

"I miss the sea with all my heart, but life is not so bad here. The slowspeakers feed us and play with us. You'll learn that life goes on, no matter where you are or who you are with. We need to make the most of life and be accepting of what befalls us. There are a few of the feeders that I really enjoy seeing everyday. If they didn't come we would probably all die of boredom."

The other female agreed. Serena was confused. How were they going to get back to the sea? Serena looked to the third dolphin and found it was another young female, two years old.

"Serena," she said to introduce herself. "I am Mornea, daughter of Alona. I was born here."

"Born here? Not at Sea?"

"No, I have never seen the sea, though mother sings of it often. What was it you said of the sea, Mother?"

Alona began to trill a beautiful Epic of life at sea filling Serena's heart with so much longing she felt it would burst.

The Sea of life, the ebb and the flow,
The ocean tides bring the future unknown
Free as the wind that whips up the waves,
The vast open blue, our hearts it craves.
We travel the sea so far and wide,
No walls or barriers but the sand and the sky.

We ride the waves and run the bore,
We sing songs and pass our lore.
We are the bird spotters and fish catchers,
We are the shark killers and crab snatchers,
We veil ourselves in waters clear,
We move in silence, all things we hear.
We shall live on without fear.
Freedom of Heart will never disappear.

As Alona finished her song the slowspeakers approached with more food. The song had stirred a longing in Serena to return to the sea, so she ate from their hands, knowing she would need strength to survive the trials ahead.

CHAPTER 12

Sea Wolves

Neo, Ridge, and Relm continued swimming south. Neo had not spoken for several days. He could not believe what had happened. After all they had gone through slowspeakers had killed Serena. Neo mournfully swam behind the two girls. Relm looked at him, worried because he hadn't eaten.

"Neo," she softly trilled as she slowed her pace, "I know how you felt about her. I loved her too. But we must go on and get home. You are the only one who knows the way now."

Neo ignored her and turned his head away. It hurt him to think that Serena would never again see the beautiful waters of BrightWater. She would never be with her nursery again or be a true matriarch. He wanted to be with her now.

Ridge turned and trilled, "Come on, Relm. I hear dolphins ahead. Let's catch up and find out if they are on a hunt."

The three dolphins picked up speed and Neo perked up a little, curious about the dolphins ahead. It was an enormous group of animals, several hundred at least. They were not Pacific bottlenose dolphins. They were Pacific white-sided dolphins, a smaller species of dolphin that were easily identifiable by the white stripes on their sides and short beaked rostrums. Most distinguishing of all were their black beaks and black shadowy eyes. The Pacific white-sides were almost half the size Neo.

"Let's swim along side them and towards the back. They know these waters better than us. They'll lead us to a great hunt in no time." Ridge predicted.

Neo enjoyed watching these little dolphins as they swam and played with each other. They were very athletic. Their smaller bodies allowed them to be acrobatic. These dolphins were energetic and quite active. Neo watched them as they frequently played by leaping, belly flopping, and somersaulting. But he did not join in. He did not feel that he had the energy to play. The entire group traveled south all day, not once stopping to feed.

"When are they going to hunt?" Relm questioned with an impatient raspberry sound. "I wonder if we should leave them and get some fish before the light goes down."

"We should stay with them." Neo piped in.

Ridge looked over at him surprised that he was talking again.

"They will eventually lead us to food, a herd this size can't travel together unless they know of huge hunts. Plus, by staying with them we'll be protected and well hid from sharks."

Ridge took Neo's opinion into consideration and agreed that it made sense. "That sounds like something Serena would say."

Neo's prediction was proved correct after Black fell. The white-sides had led the bottlenose to a squid buffet. As the squid rose from the deep following the phytoplankton, the dolphins gorged upon them all night long. The next morning the entire herd was well fed and feeling good. Within the large company of dolphins there were many smaller troupes. These small groups of males, friends, or mothers and calves, celebrated the morning with amazing spinning and flipping. As the day wore on the dolphins began resting. They all felt very safe in this large herd, which is why it took several seconds to realize that a warning call was being shouted out. From the very back of the company a cry pierced through the dolphin chatter and sent the white-sides blasting forwards.

Ridge called to Neo and Relm. "Stay close together, and stay with the herd."

The bottlenose squished in with the other dolphins forming a tightly packed bundle. Neo's eyes tried to focus through the crowd of black and white dolphins. When all the dolphins were tightly packed, their coloration made it difficult to distinguish individual animals. The warning calls were louder now and all the white-sides were turning their heads trying to see behind them and still swim quickly forward.

"What is going on?" Relm trilled.

"Is it a large shark?" Neo questioned.

"No," Ridge whistled, "If a large shark was stalking us we would know by now and it would have given up the moment we reacted to it."

"Maybe a skywhale?" Relm trilled as she pushed in closer to the white-side next to her.

"No," whistled Neo, "I don't hear one."

The white-sided dolphins suddenly changed direction as a loud popping sound came from the left. Relm cast out through the muddled black and white patterns of the dolphins and an image came to her that she wasn't able to see with her eyes. The images of many dolphins passed before her but there was something else. Something huge. Neo and Ridge cast out as well and realized that through the jumble of black and white, orcas were flanking the group, from behind and on either side. The orcas were mostly black, with white bellies and a large white patch just behind their black eyes.

"Killers! They must have been trailing us!" Ridge chirped. "They probably were waiting for a white-side to lag behind."

"That warning call must have been from a dolphin who cast them," Relm said desperately. "What are we going to do?"

"We don't have to worry much about the killers because they usually don't hunt our kind," Neo hoped.

"But now we're mixed up with white-sides!" Ridge countered. "Killers normally prey on them. If we try to break away, the killers will grab us for sure."

Neo's heart began to pound as he cast the eighteen foot long, twelve thousand pound whales. He remembered Epics being sung about the killer whales, the top predator of the sea. They were as intelligent and as crafty as dolphins, only twenty times their weight and strength. Some orcas, who remained residents of a home range, ate mostly fish and squid. But transients traveled long distances and fed on large marine mammals. They ate animals as small as a baby sea lion and as large as the huge gray whales.

"I've heard Epics about killers," Neo chirped. The girls pressed in even closer as the killer whales flanked all sides of the company.

"No one can out run them, and they do not tire. They talk, but we can't understand their dialects. And they are smart too."

"Neo, stop it. I don't want to hear about them." Relm was starting to shake.

Ridge looked over at Neo. "I've heard they are amazing hunters," she had an edge of admiration in her chirps. "Each one knows their job before the hunt even begins. They know how their prey will react to every move they make. Killers like to tease their prey and will sometimes play with their food before finally killing it and eating it."

"Ridge!" shrieked Relm. "You are talking about us! We are their prey!"

"I didn't say it was a good thing."

The Orcas began popping their jaws towards the dolphins. They fought to control their panic. Neo looked around. There were several hundred dolphins, but if one panicked and tried to swim for safety, the killers waiting along the edges would chase that dolphin down until they caught up with him, or the dolphin was too exhausted to swim any more.

"Stay close," Ridge whistled. "Do not give in to fear. Push into the center."

The bottlenose pushed their way deeper into the group. The dolphins struggled through the others to the surface to grab a breath of air.

Out of the blue a cry filled the water as a white-sided dolphin was rammed by a killer whale in the back of the herd. Neo heard her cries but knew he could not help. All the dolphins packed closer together. Two orcas swam back and forth on either side taunting the dolphins, trying to scare one out of the herd. Neo realized that the killer whales were driving them as he would herd a school of fish. And when the fish circle becomes tightened the next step in the hunt is to swim in and feed.

"Ridge!" Neo cried. "We are not safe here! We need to move towards the front of the herd!"

"We're right in the middle!" Ridge argued. "They won't come for us in here."

"Think about it!" Neo squeaked. "We are now the circled fish!"

All of a sudden an orca rammed straight into the center of the group. Dolphins went flying in all directions. Relm, Ridge, and Neo were slammed backward as other dolphins came falling through the water towards them.

This created the effect the orca wanted. Chaos. Most of the white-sides struggled to reform ranks, and get back in the group, but some were too frightened or stunned to react quickly enough. The killer whales rushed in to attack the stragglers. Several orcas were pursuing dolphins that swam away from the group. Relm and Neo recovered quickly, but Ridge had been hit very hard in the head by a rammed dolphin. A killer whale was echolocating her.

"No!" Neo cried, as he realized Ridge was targeted.

Relm swam towards Ridge and screamed at her, "Come on! Fly Away! Now! Ridge, follow me! Ridge!"

Ridge came to her senses and bolted forward, following Relm. They were headed back into the large company when a killer whale appeared right behind her. The killer whale sent out a warning call. It was a mournful sounding elongated squeak that began low and ascended in pitch. Relm and Ridge blasted forward but the whale was coming up fast behind. The large orca opened her mouth and almost had Ridge's tail close enough to grab.

"Save, save, save!!" Neo cried.

Neo came blasting in from the side and rammed the orca hard with his rostrum. It was like ramming into a rock. But the orca was distracted and turned to look at Neo as Ridge and Relm made it into the herd and swam towards the front.

Neo and the orca locked eyes for a split second and then the orca opened her mouth and showed Neo her enormous teeth. Neo's eyes widened in fear. He knew he could never out run the orca if he tried to turn and swim away. So he swam straight towards the orca's face and jumped right over her head. The orca leaped up to catch him but he cleared her and headed for the herd. Other killer whales had been attracted to the commotion.

"Oh no!" Neo trilled.

He must have made them really mad. Now he was being tailed by several orcas. Neo continuously leaped out of the water to gain speed. The killer whales were just as fast. They clicked madly at him as he flew through the water. The large orca opened her mouth to try to catch Neo by the tail. His flukes brushed up against her teeth and they cut his skin. Neo found strength he never knew he had. Gathering up all his might, Neo pushed harder and swam faster than he ever had. He was right behind the herd of white-sides. He burst into the air and dove head first into the tightly packed dolphins. He was in! But he didn't know if the offended orcas would give up so easily. With the killers just behind them, the white-sided dolphins pushed forward. Neo looked on either side of him. The Orcas flanked the group.

'They're not giving up.' Neo thought. He continued to leap into the air trying to find Relm and Ridge.

CHAPTER 13

Freedom Spirit

As the days and weeks passed on Serena learned everything her mother had gone through the past two years.

"I was very sick when I beached. I felt terrible sadness leaving Seris behind. But I knew you would take care of him, Serena. The slowspeakers brought me here. I was all alone for many Lights and Blacks before a new dolphin joined me. Alona came in nearly full with calf. She was malnourished and had lost a lot of weight. I now had purpose in my life, to help Alona.

"I improved quickly and busied myself with tending Alona and helping her prepare for the calf. Only I could cast Alona and tell her that the baby was growing and getting stronger within her as the slowspeakers fed her. I started to eat so well that the slowspeakers no longer raised me up out of the water.

"Finally, Alona's calf was born a perfect healthy female. Alona named her Mornea in honor of the perfect morning she was born."

Siren told Serena that other dolphins would come for awhile and then they would be taken out again. She did not know where they went. Serena was very curious about this. Where did the other dolphins go? To another slowspeaker holder? To die? Serena learned from Mornea that slowspeakers could communicate through body language, so she set herself to learning how to communicate with them. Serena watched as a slowspeaker moved its hands in a strange gesture and Mornea would take off and do a beautiful jump. The human sounded a whistle and Mornea swam up to the edge of the pool and would receive fish.

"Certain hand movements mean to do something," Mornea excitedly explained, "and if you do it, you get fish!"

"We get fish anyway," Serena reasoned, "Why should we do anything for it?"

"Because its more fun than doing nothing at all, and I feel like I've earned it."

Serena thought about this and she was surprised by the calf's wisdom. Hunting was earning the food. And by learning to understand the slowspeakers, she would earn hers as well. The more she understood their signals, the more food she would get.

Serena caught on to the game very quickly, and learned the hand signals' meanings just by watching the other dolphin's training sessions. She learned the signals for jumping, whistling, rolling over, and laying still. She learned to copy the slowspeakers behaviors. If they splashed her, she would splash back. If they danced around, she would dance around.

Serena was almost completely healed now. Serena and Siren became inseparable. Serena sometimes felt like a calf again being taken care of by her loving mother. The slowspeakers seemed to catch on to their connection and fed them together. Serena had been in this pool for almost four months, both she and Siren were in perfect health.

Serena's desire to return to the sea was growing more and more intense everyday.

Siren told her, "Do not mourn the sea but cherish it, my dear. We may never be able to swim as far as we please or feel the thrill of the hunt, but we have each other, and that is enough for me. We are alive."

But it wasn't enough for Serena. And she was generally very bored. She took to inventing games for herself like tossing her fish around the pool pretending she was after a live fish, and hiding her fish around the pool so she could stalk her prey. She spent her days remembering her adventure across the world and back again. Almost starving in the ocean desert only to come across a beautiful oasis with more food then she could ever eat; attacking the shark that had tried to kill Relm; learning the secrets of the sponge dolphins; leaving the dolphins that begged for food; saving the whitemelon from the nets; watching the massacre of the sharks; surfing the waves in warm waters halfway across the Pacific; and riding the whales all the way home.

Almost home. She had been so close. She hoped that Neo led the way so Ridge and Relm would come to see BrightWater. She missed Neo dearly. She would love to see his bright eyes appear before her carrying a piece of sea weed in his mouth, squeaking,

"Come and catch me, if you can!"

Serena was overjoyed when a large leaf fell into the pool on a windy day. She tossed the leaf around for hours with Mornea, teaching her to play capture the sea weed. Serena carried the leaf around for a few days before the slowspeaker took it out of the pool.

Serena looked forward to the slowspeaker visits. Only when they came would she get fed. She learned to enjoy the sound of the slowspeaker's whistle, because it meant food, or toys, or something was on the way. Serena would spend hours looking over the pool wall waiting for someone to walk by so she could splash them or make sounds to bring them over. Serena found she could control the behavior of the slowspeakers by cooing at them as if they were calves. They would rush over and give her food or play games with her, like chase or hide and seek. The slowspeaker would sometimes run around the pool and Serena would chase after them as if she was hunting, or the slowspeaker would duck behind the wall and pop up to surprise her. Serena had unwillingly settled into a nice routine; playing, sleeping, eating. Feeling completely safe was something Serena became accustomed to. She was fully relaxed knowing no predators could find her here.

One morning however, things seemed different. Serena couldn't say why, but she was anxious. She felt a change was coming. Siren felt it also and when the slowspeakers did not arrive with the morning meal, the dolphins began to get nervous.

"What is that sound? Do you hear?"

A low rumbling had begun.

"The water is dropping! Look!"

Mornea began swimming frantically around the pool as the water line slowly lowered. Siren jumped out of the water to see if she could find out what was going on.

"They are moving us! They have the holders and lots of slowspeakers around. They are going to move us!"

"Are they moving all of us?" Alona squeaked.

"I do not know."

As the water became only a few feet deep it became more difficult for the dolphins to move about. The slowspeakers entered the pool and targeted Siren first. As Serena watched helplessly they surrounded her and put their hands on her. They slipped Siren inside the cloth sling and lifted her awkwardly out of the pool.

Siren cried out as she left, "My dear friend, Alona, if we never meet again, know that I love you and Mornea. I shall never forget you and will sing of you and your miracle until the end of my days. My daughter, Serena, I love you forever."

She disappeared over the wall.

Serena cried out, "Mother, mother!"

Her cries went unheeded. A few minutes later the slowspeakers reentered the water and captured Serena in the stretcher.

"Serena," Alona cried, "You are going with Siren, tell her I love her also."

"Goodbye, Mornea. Goodbye, Alona. I will miss you where ever I go. I'll never forget you," Serena squeaked through her blowhole as she was lifted over the wall.

Once again Serena felt gravity's pull as her weight pushed down on her lungs making every breath difficult. She could not see around her but she felt herself being lifted and then placed down on the soft mat.

She heard her mother close by. "Serena! Serena!"

"I'm here. It's Serena. I'm right next to you."

"Wherever we go next, Serena, remember I'll always love you."

After that Serena could not hear her anymore. A loud rumbling noise filled Serena's ears as the truck they were laying in began to move. Serena had forgotten how uncomfortable the first trip had been. The rough, bumpy ride sent vibrations throughout Serena's body making her head and stomach ache. The slowspeakers were pouring cool water over her skin and rubbing her affectionately. It was hard for Serena to concentrate but she wondered briefly where she was going and if she would be with her mother or not.

After a long while, the truck stopped bumping and grumbling and Serena sensed motion all around her. She was once again lifted and this time she was lowered into a small pool. Serena began to inwardly panic. This pool was so small that Serena couldn't move. She cast in front of her and received an echo back so fast that she jolted a bit. The pool was only a few feet deep and just wide enough to fit her flippers. The end of her beak was touching the container wall in front of her. She felt her tail flukes brush against the wall behind her. Claustrophobia began to set in but Serena had no escape.

She closed her eyes and began to sing to herself of the wide open sea, imagining no walls, no barriers, just open ocean as far as she could cast. Her whistles and buzzes were so soft that she didn't think anyone heard her. Serena's tiny pool was sitting on the deck of a large boat. She felt vibrations in her ears again as the boat motor started. The water in the tank began to slosh back and forth as the boat chugged out of the marina. Serena held back her panic, she sat as still as a dead dolphin and breathing very little. She did not want to think about where she might be going now or where her mother might be.

She remembered Neo. She remembered Ridge and Relm too. She hoped they had all made it to safe waters. She hoped they had found other dolphins to hunt with. Serena rested half of her mind for a while and thought of nothing. She became fully aware when the boat motor changed sounds as if they were slowing down. Serena sensed a great deal of commotion around her as the boat came to a halt. Suddenly there were slowspeakers all around her. Serena rolled an eye upwards and recognized one of the slowspeakers who played with her often. There were many she did not recognize. They reached their long arms out towards her. She felt many hands touching her and reaching under her belly. She was lifted out of the tub and placed in a stretcher again. Her vision was blocked by the canvas so that she could not see where she was going. She suddenly felt helpless again, lost and afraid. She felt alone and emotions flooded her mind. She felt herself shaking and closed her eyes.

"Mother," Serena cried.

Serena continued the soft squeaking as she felt herself being lifted. Serena struggled to contain her panic as it welled up within her. She felt unbalanced as the stretcher leaned to one side, the slowspeakers had moved to one side of the stretcher. Serena remembered this is what happened just before she was lowered into the pool. She braced herself for a fall and just as she predicted one side of the stretcher was dropped and she plunged down into cool water.

Disoriented, Serena cast around to find out where she was. She expected to immediately feel the echo of a black wall. But she did not receive that echo. Instead she saw fish and sand and plants and openness. She was in the ocean! Serena cast and looked around her taking in all in. Her skin felt the different texture of the ocean water, her mouth tasted the sea salt. She dove to the bottom and felt the sand on her belly. Happiness filled her heart and she jetted to the surface with as much speed as she could muster and burst through the water in pure joy, feeling the cool air in her face. She splashed back down tickled by the sensation of not worrying about walls or floors. She oriented herself towards the southeast, to swim away from the boat. But she stopped. What about her mother? Where was she? Didn't she come along? Serena leaped out of the water along side the boat to look for her on the deck. The slowspeakers were carrying a stretcher towards the water.

Serena swam to the back of the boat and called, "Mother! Mother!"

Serena leaped again looking at the people carrying the filled stretcher knowing what her mother was feeling in there.

"Mother, everything is going to be alright! I'm here, we're going home!"

She did not know if her mother heard her so she continued circling around the stern of the boat.

Finally, a disoriented dolphin fell back into the sea with an ungraceful splash. Siren cast about and became oriented realizing that she was in the ocean. After being away for almost three years she was overwhelmed by the vastness of space around her. Had Serena not been there with her she might have panicked, but Serena came to her and gave her a gentle, reassuring rub.

"Come with me, Mom. I know the way home. Everyone is waiting for us."

Siren looked to Serena for support, and as memories flooded her thoughts she softly squeaked to Serena, "I remember. I remember all the friends I left behind. I never thought I'd see them again; Alatina, Radill…" she suddenly burst out, "Seris!"

"I remember the feel of the rushing water in my face swimming as fast as I can, as far as I want to go."

Serena saw a change in Siren's eyes. Disorientation was replaced by elation. They were free. They were alive. They were going home. Serena and Siren leaped together looking back at the boat where the slowspeakers were waving their arms and shouting. Serena heard the slowspeakers' high pitched whistle blow that always meant something good was to follow. She jumped in the air as high as she could one last time, then took off at top speed with her mother beside her headed straight for home.

They had not eaten yet that day, however, and Serena began looking for something to eat. Serena easily switched into hunting mode even though she had not had the need to hunt for many months. All her instincts returned to her and the thrill of the hunt began to course through her veins. Siren, however, had not hunted in many years, and Serena knew she felt nervous and unsure about her skills as a hunter.

"Don't worry, Mother, I'm here, and I love you. You'll remember everything soon enough. You are in control out here. You have nothing to fear. Do you see all those fish down there?"

Siren looked down at the teeming fish below her, zipping in and out of the rocks and kelp.

"Those fish fear you. You are the top. You are the predator. You are the hunter. They fear you, and they should. Because you are about to kill them, and eat them all."

Siren's heart began to pound. Her eyes widened.

"You go below them and scare them to the top, I'll surround them and make the fish turn into a ball, then you come charging in to take the first feed. Ready, Mom?"

Siren was silent. Then she looked at Serena and opened her mouth menacingly. "I can feel hunger, Serena. Not just a hunger for food, but a hunger to hunt, a hunger to play the game."

"The game?"

"The game of life and death."

Siren dove down and made a swooping circle to gather up the fish. The fish who had been watching apprehensively from below panicked and raced into a protective ball. Siren pushed them upwards as Serena raced around them, whistling and blowing bubbles at them. The terrified fish corralled themselves tightly together, and Siren darted in to take the first few. Serena was right behind her, and they fed until they were full.

"I remember how it feels to be a dolphin again, daughter. How it is to be independent and self sufficient. You are now grown up and fully capable of taking care of yourself. I'm proud of you, Serena."

Serena didn't know what to say. She thought about how much she had missed her mother the past few years. She remembered a question she wanted to ask that she felt only her mother would be able to answer.

She asked very matter-of-factly, "Mother, how will I be able to know which male will provide a healthy calf?"

Siren looked surprised, but seemed was very glad to instruct her daughter.

"Well, Serena, the first thing you want to look for is a healthy male. Health is the most important; it will assure a healthy calf. Next, you should look for a male that is strong, perhaps a dominant male. The most dominant are called Alphas. That will assure a strong calf. And lastly, look for a male that is wise. This will ensure a wise calf. Although any calf of yours is sure to wise, Serena."

Serena thought about it a while and determined she would settle for nothing less than an Alpha male as the father of her calf. They swam in silence for most of the day, content, full, and eager to get home.

CHAPTER 14

Serena's Epic Song

Serena knew they were close. She began to recognize certain features in the waters. Siren was remembering more and more every day. She was able to hunt and navigate through the cool Pacific waters that she left just three years earlier. Serena was excited and worried. Had Neo, Ridge, and Relm made it home? Would she be able to find them? How would they react to her coming home after they left her in the hands of the slowspeakers? She wasn't sure what to expect, but she wanted to find her nursery group more than anything else. She wanted to see Seris and Alatina. She wanted her mother to be accepted back into the group. She wanted to tell her story so that her nursery group would not suffer the same fate as the dolphins who perished in the Tangler. Serena and Siren were so eager to get into home range waters that they didn't stop to eat all day. They just kept swimming, finding faster currents and riding the waves of the shoreline parallel to the shore.

Finally, they followed the curve of the California Peninsula up into the Sea of Cortez. Serena knew this part of the ocean as well as her own name. This was BrightWater. She recognized every boulder and sandy patch. Siren was getting very excited, yet she was nervous about coming home after being away for so long. Would the other dolphins accept her? Would they understand what she's been through?

Serena began calling out through the water, the familiar sound of her own name, six alternating high and low whistles, "Serena!"

Siren began to do the same, calling out her name.

After a while Siren chirped, "I hope our friends hear us, and realize we're back."

For hours mother and daughter called out into the vast waters.

At long last Serena heard a reply, "Aleta is here!"

"Serena is here!" she screamed.

Serena and Siren picked up speed in the direction of the calls. It was Aleta, Alatina's daughter. She was about a half a mile away. Serena and Siren raced towards her, Serena's heart pounding with anticipation. Aleta came into view, her eyes wide with surprise.

"Serena is that really you? Siren? Siren?! How? How?"

Serena and Aleta greeted each other with full body rubs, Aleta rubbed Siren's flipper.

"Where have you been all this time? Siren, you're alive!"

"I'll explain everything once we reach Alatina," Siren whistled. "How far is she?"

"Not far, not far. Follow me."

As they swam Aleta explained that she was out scouting when she heard Serena's call.

"After we discovered you were gone, Alatina searched for hours before giving up and getting the group to safety. Seris wouldn't eat for days after we lost you. Finally, Alatina made him eat. We turned west and headed out to sea. Alatina didn't want to go too far South. The storm ended soon after and then we came back home. We thought that if you had survived you would come home. When you never returned we assumed you had perished. Where have you both been all this time?"

Serena was silent for a while, then answered, "I had something I needed to do before I came home, and I have so much to tell everyone, an Epic."

Siren looked at Serena searchingly. Serena had not told her of the Epic yet. Aleta called forward to the other dolphins with great excitement. She turned to Serena and Siren.

"Don't make a sound. I want this to be a surprise. They won't know you're here until they cast you, and they probably won't believe it until they see it," Aleta squeaked.

After several more minutes Serena began to hear distant calls. The nursery group was answering Aleta's calls. They had found them! After two years of separation she was finally home with her nursery group, and bringing her mother home made their reunion even more remarkable. A few seconds before she saw them Serena cast upon the familiar dolphins. A riot of squeaks and trills filled her ears as the dolphins came into view. Everyone was still together; Ana, Anu, Radill, Ravis, Tinen, Seris, and Alatina, plus a dolphin Serena had not met yet. The dolphins rushed at her giving her body rubs and pectoral flipper slaps. Suddenly all the dolphins seemed to realize at once who Serena was accompanied by.

"Siren," Siren whistled her signature whistle.

The dolphins were silent in awe. Alatina came forward.

"Siren. We missed you. We are glad to have you back with us at last."

With those words of acceptance and welcome the other dolphins flung themselves upon Siren in greeting. Young Seris appeared through the group.

"Mother? Is that you?"

"Seris, my son. You've grown so much my dear. I missed you."

Seris still did not seem quite sure.

He cast her a few times and then asked, "Where did you go?"

Everyone was silent waiting for the answer.

Serena came forward, "We'll tell you everything soon. We have amazing adventures to tell you of, and Epics to sing. But I want to know how all of you have been. Seris, tell us what you have done to get so big this year."

The eleven dolphins gabbed and talked for hours without stopping. Serena met Ravis's baby, named Radisa. She was a perfect little girl. Serena learned that the group was able to make it back to the home waters before the baby was born. The dolphins listened in awe to Serena as she told them of her adventures and struggles to make it home.

Then Alatina asked, "But we were told that you went onto a beach and you were attacked by slowspeakers. We thought you were dead. Until that moment I had never given up hope of your return. How is it that both you and Siren survived beaching and slowspeakers?"

Serena was about to go into a long story, but she stopped and asked, "Who told you I had beached? Who told you I was attacked?" Serena squeaked.

"Two young dolphins came around one day with a small nursery group. They discovered we were your nursery school and told us of your fate. They seemed very sad to tell us and they swam away. Did they know you well?"

Two dolphins? What about the third? Who was missing?

"Alatina, were the dolphins male or female?"

"Female, of course."

Where was Neo? Did he not make it back? Serena tried to remember her last memories of him.

"Neo, go back. You can make it home, to BrightWater. You can live and form an alliance and be strong, the strongest dolphin who swam across the ocean and back again."

"No, Serena, I am only strong because of you. And if you are going to stay up here and dry out, so am I. I won't leave you, Serena. I love you."

"Go back!"

"No!"

The clear images of their parting flooded Serena's mind as she saw Neo being pushed out into the waves.

"Serena, I'll miss you!"

"I love you too."

Serena's heart fell. If Neo had perished that day she would never forgive herself. She had to find Ridge and Relm. She had to know what had happened.

"Serena, are you alright?"

Alatina and Siren were looking at her concerned.

"Yes," Serena answered, "But I have just realized that my journey is not over until I find my friends. Alatina, where did you speak with the two young dolphins?"

Alatina gazed at Serena for a moment.

"Serena, I see leadership and power within you. I see an age beyond years and I know that you are no longer part of my nursery. You are a matriarch of your own school now, and it seems you have some hidden wisdom to share.

"Come with me, Serena. We will all go find your friends."

Alatina lead the way. Serena looked back to see Seris swimming along side Siren rubbing her flipper occasionally. Siren looked happier than she'd ever seen her. Not joyous, but content. She was where she belonged. Serena had always thought that coming home would make her feel that way. But for some reason, it didn't. She did not feel like she was where she belonged. She felt as if the journey was not completed. She did not feel home yet.

Serena followed Alatina feeling some urgency while at the same time afraid of what she might discover. After some searching Serena heard in the distance the familiar calls of Ridge and Relm. Alatina was calling out to their matriarch. As the nursery group approached Serena called out her distinguishable signature whistle, six alternating high and low whistles. Ridge and Relm looked at each other in disbelief, but only for a second. They rounded on Serena, filling the water with whistles and trills, and rubbing Serena with affection on her flippers and back. The three dolphins wrestled awhile, and gabbed on and on about how Serena survived and how long it took to finally make it home.

"Neo was the one who took charge after you left, Serena. He was the one who knew the way home," Relm trilled. "We were lost for the first few days, Neo wouldn't speak at all. And we were afraid to speak to him."

"We were afraid that Sorrow had taken him over. But Relm snapped him out it."

"I didn't, really. The killers are the ones who woke him up."

"Killers?" whistled Serena.

"We were traveling with white-sides when a pack of killers attacked. Neo risked his life to save mine," Ridge bubbled. "The killers were very upset about it and chased Neo for hours."

Serena listened with dread growing in her heart.

"And, where is Neo now?"

Relm and Ridge gave each other meaningful glances.

"Follow us, Serena." Relm whistled.

Worried at what her friends were going to show her, Serena left behind her nursery group and followed her friends some ways out to sea. Did Neo survive the killer whale onslaught? Maybe he survived but was injured? Soon she would know, and she was afraid of what she would find out.

Serena, Ridge, and Relm were several miles offshore when a large group of males were suddenly upon them. A group of at least ten big males surrounded them and jeered at them. The male dolphin societies were very complex. Males formed alliances and fought for dominance. The top dolphin is the alpha male. The middle of a marauding male group was not the place a female dolphin would normally want to be.

Serena asked herself why Ridge and Relm would bring her here. What did these males have to do with Neo? A fearful thought entered her mind that Neo may have been killed by this group of dolphins, and anger welled up within her. She looked around at the dolphins that surrounded her. Many had large rakes across their backs and bite marks on their tails and dorsal fins. These animals did not look like they would have any hesitation beating each other to a pulp, so Serena supposed they would have no qualms with attacking strangers. A big dolphin with a gash on the side of his face swam forward.

"Hello, leaving the nursery looking for some fun? Little ladies shouldn't come out this far all alone."

"We are not alone," Serena said bravely, "We are together, and if you want to fight, I have to tell you, the three of us have seen more in our short lives then you will ever see, and have survived more terrors than you can imagine. So, if you think that we are going to suffer an ugly bully like yourself, I'll have to show you the meaning suffering."

And with that Serena turned head over tail so fast that the ugly brute didn't even flinch before Serena whacked him in the head with her flukes. A mighty battle broke out. Serena, Ridge, and Relm might have had a tough time of it, but a familiar whistle sounded sending the other males swimming towards it. The whistle was familiar but it sounded more commanding and powerful than before. The males all turned back toward the females in formation behind their leader, the alpha male. There was a short silence as the females and males faced each other.

Serena felt herself being cast and heard the Alpha chirp, "Serena?"

Serena recognized the voice immediately and the figure before her was as familiar to her as her own self. It was Neo. Neo was the dolphin at the head of the pack and in his astonishment at seeing Serena he forgot the other males were even there.

"Serena. Serena, is that you?"

Serena's posture softened. She said his name first, absorbed in the fact that one of her friends, seemingly lost, was before her again.

"Neo. Neo, I'm home."

Neo tentatively approached Serena and turned on his side and rubbed her flipper. Serena's and Neo's eyes locked, and the memories of their great adventure flooded back. Serena cooed at him, and Neo side rubbed her, and belly rubbed her, and swam all about her. Neo gave out a great whistle and together they suddenly soared for the surface. They leapt from the water in celebration with amazing strength and sent a great spray of water as they spun through the air. Neo's squeaks were higher pitched then usual in his excitement.

"I can't believe you made it home! How did you escape? Where have you been all this time? I never thought I'd see you again!"

Then as if just realizing other dolphins were around, Neo turned to group of males.

"This is Serena, the dolphin I sang about. She is the one who helped me when I escaped from the net, nearly starved, fought off a great white, rescued a white melon, and rode the whales back to shore. She is the one who the slowspeakers caught and it appears that she escaped from them again."

Neo arched his back and flexed his tail.

"And any dolphin who tries to mess with her will have to deal with me."

Then Neo, without warning, smashed his rostrum into the side of the ugly scarred male as an example to the others. The other alliances took off so as not to be in the way if Neo decided to show off his dominance again. Neo spent the rest of the day with Serena, Ridge, and Relm sharing stories of what had happened in the past year.

"The killers followed the white-sides for hours and killed eight of them before they moved on. I swam through the middle of the company hoping to blend into the black and white clutter, but the killers watched me closely, I thought I was a goner.

"I finally caught up to Relm and Ridge at the front. Once the killers were gone, we left the white-sides and traveled home."

"Neo really took charge after that." Ridge trilled. "He was driven, he wanted to get home. But just as we were rounding the shore into BrightWater, that group of males attacked us."

Relm cut in, "Ridge and Neo fought them hard, and Neo beat the alpha. Then Neo started boasting to them of our journey, and the males were fascinated."

Ridge bubbled as if this were a big joke. "Neo is now known as the most aggressive and strong of them all, he is feared and respected. His Epics are the greatest stories the other dolphins have ever heard, and they love listening to him tell the stories of fighting the sharks, killers, and slowspeakers. The battle scar on his tail from the killer is famous."

Relm laughed, "He is the leader of the most wayward group of males around."

"We are explorers, not wayward, and we've helped you girls out several times."

Neo told Serena that he was referring to a few times sharks had been in the area and his alliance chased them out, and times they had joined in hunting parties. As for Serena, she was so proud of him. He had grown so much from when she had first met him. He was stronger, bigger, and wiser than he had been.

"So, Serena," Neo asked late in the day, "What are your plans? What will you do now?"

Serena thought awhile before she answered.

"I think that I will form my own nursery school with young females and new mothers. You'll join, of course?" Serena asked Ridge and Relm.

"Of course!" they cried.

"I want to teach other dolphins all that I have learned so far on our journey. I want to teach calves how to hunt and how to be safe. And I want to sing them the Epic."

Neo stopped in the water.

"The Epic. So you have one then. Let's hear it, Serena."

"Yes, Serena," cried Ridge and Relm, "Sing us the Epic."

Serena's mind flooded with memories of the Tanglers that killed the dolphins, the drift Tangler, the hooks that took the sharks, the blasters at the shrimp boat and at the fish trap. She recalled the polluted water behind the cruise ship and the dolphins that were fed fish by slowspeaker hands. She remembered her rescue from the beach and the walls and the whistles. She remembered an encounter with a little girl swimming at the surface so peacefully. Serena took a breath at the surface and began to sing.

❧   ❧   ❧

Several years later, dusk was upon the ocean sending streaks of pink and orange across the surface. Serena lay still resting a few feet below looking at her group. The other seven dolphins looked anxiously at their matriarch for an evening Epic. Relm and Ridge and their sons sat waiting. A young female named Mysti had joined the group, and Siren, Serena's mother, was there too. After Seris was old enough to leave the nursery group Siren moved over to Serena's school. Serena's calf, sired by Neo, was a little girl named Serenity, whom Serena loved more than anything else in the world.

Serena often sang of motherhood as Alatina used to do. She also sang of the hunt and teamwork. Tonight everyone wanted to listen because she was going to again tell a great tale of nets and sharks and whales. And she began with her own song, The Epic of the Slowspeakers. It opened with songs about how to survive Tanglers and how inspect skywhales for danger. It told of slowspeakers who gave fish and how dolphins should not accept it in place of hunting. Serena sang to the dolphins of harmless humans in the water, and dangerous predators in their skywhales. The last verse of the Epic reflected her experiences. Other dolphins gathered around as Serena sang:

There you see a little body floating at the surface.
Little movement, quiet sound, at first they seem helpless.
Big eyes, long arms; making sound, but not much,
Their eyes speak, just like yours; they play, they touch.

In some places they are feeders, usurpers, exploiters, destroyers.
Netting, hooking, beating, biting, trawling, cutting, killing.
Fearless, hunters, they net and hook fish, shrimp, sharks.

Brutal, they kill all. They do not care what you are.
The thunder crack means watch your back.
The bitter water means large skywhales.
The drop of a net will surely mean death,
So swim away fast as the rushing gales.

On the beach you may find life renewed.
Slowspeakers have come to the rescue.
They fill your stomach and surround you with walls.
Being alone is the worst part of all.
But soon you are strong again to play and fight.
And splashing a slowspeaker was my secret delight.
Games and whistles, but the Ocean I never forgot.
Some will return and some will not.

Kindness, playfulness, generous, patient.
Slowspeakers are a mixture and each one is different.
They are individuals, like you and I,
The young and the old, different as earth and sky.
What are they? Playful yet killers, so are we too.
But they waste and they squander, we take a different view.
Never take in excess from others, nor try to change their way of life.
Do not hope to control other beings, nor stop them from learning to survive.
Forever remember the lessons I sing,
Pass on your knowledge, you have so much to bring.
Love every being for their purpose and for what they give.
In this world, all creatures then, in harmony shall live."

Serena's Epic spread through the oceans as fast as sound would travel. Dolphins who listened to her would tell others and so on, until the Epic traveled around the sea. Dolphins added their own knowledge to the Epic until it became the largest and most sung Epic to traverse the oceans. Several years later Serena heard her Epic with all the knowledge of even distant dolphins and knew her journey was worth it. Dolphins knew about slowspeakers, and they were safer because of this.

Serena's calf was now three years old. Serenity finally had the freedom to swim unbound to her nursery. She was becoming quite a fine scout. As she swam out into the infinite sea Serenity encountered a small boat with a little boy peering over the side. She had heard the Epic many times and knew about humans. Serenity surfaced, and looked up at the boy to get a close look at the creature she had heard so much about. As she looked at him, he looked back. Their eyes connected and they looked at each other in mutual understanding and intelligence. Serenity's gaze reflected the knowledge she had gained from her mother. Indeed, every human who looks upon a dolphin that has heard Serena's Epic, will feel that relaxed dolphin gaze reveal the thought, "I know you."

Just as the boy tried to reach out and touch her, Serenity disappeared beneath the waves.

0-595-31406-6

Printed in the United States
42330LVS00005B/299